A SPRITE CHRISTMAS

THE MYSTERY HOUSE SERIES, BOOK SIXTEEN

Eva Pohler

Eva Pohler Books
20011 Park Ranch
San Antonio, Texas 78259
www.evapohler.com

Publisher's Note: This is a work of fiction. Names, characters, places, and incidents are a product of the author's imagination. Locales and public names are sometimes used for atmospheric purposes. Any resemblance to actual people, living or dead, or to businesses, companies, events, institutions, or locales is completely coincidental.

Edited by Alexis Rigoni

Book Cover Design by B Rose DesignZ

A Sprite Christmas/ Eva Pohler. -- 1st ed.

ISBN: 978-1-958390-84-9

Contents

For the casualties of civil war, especially the children.

CHAPTER ONE

Murder Ranch

Ellen stepped from the driver's seat of their rental car—a blue Chevy Onix—and joined Tanya and Sue on the edge of the gravel drive, staring up at the two-story Victorian with skepticism. "Is it really called Murder Ranch?" she asked.

"Yes, and I like it," Sue declared.

Tanya shifted uncomfortably, pulling her long, black cardigan more tightly around her. She wore leggings and running shoes, her blonde ponytail swinging as she turned toward them. "I feel underdressed next to you two. Why so fancy?"

Ellen tucked her hands into her trouser pockets. "I would've dressed differently if I'd known we were going to be squatting today."

Sue fluffed her dark bangs, her false lashes catching the afternoon sun like miniature fans. "When I dress up, I make better food choices. It's psychological. My new strategy."

Ellen raised a brow. "Is that what inspired the rhinestone blazer? I really like it, by the way."

"No," Sue said smugly. "That was divine intervention."

"You look great, Sue. You both do." Tanya looked between them, frowning. Ellen, at five-foot-ten and wearing a camel blazer with dark, wide-legged jeans and a navy, cashmere sweater, was closer to Tanya's six feet. Sue, wearing black, straight-legged trousers, a black-and-white striped top, and a black denim blazer with rhinestones on the lapel, stood at five-foot-one. "But I didn't realize we were dressing for brunch with royalty."

"You're fine," Ellen said. "Lately, I've been watching this French stylist on YouTube, Marie-Anne Lecoeur. She helps women over fifty, and, apparently, I've been wearing 'frumpy' and 'mumsy' clothes for years."

"So, this is . . ." Tanya gestured at Ellen's tweed blazer, silk scarf, and low-heeled boots.

"Elevated," Ellen said. "No more tent tops and capri pants. Turns out those make you look even bigger."

"Our boots are a major improvement on our Crocs and Stocks," Sue pointed out.

"That's exactly what Marie-Anne Lecoeur says."

Tanya looked down at herself. "I guess I'll have to level up, too, if I want to fit in with the fancy Ghost Healers."

"Please," Sue snorted. "With your perfect figure, you'd look good in a tent made of shower curtains."

"Or a Mumu woven from plastic grocery bags," Ellen added.

Tanya laughed despite herself. "Oh, stop."

Sue shook her head. "See, that's where I would have said, 'Keep going.'"

Ellen turned her attention back to the Victorian. At least as tall as it was wide, the dark brick structure, with its turret and multiple chimneys, reminded Ellen of a Bram Stoker novel. "It's bigger than I expected."

Sue stepped forward, hands on her hips, her boots crunching on the gravel. "And better."

"It's south-facing," Tanya pointed out, "which means great sunlight for front yard landscaping."

"Oh, that's true," Ellen clapped her hands. "I can't wait to go plant shopping."

Sue smiled gleefully. "Don't you just *feel* the potential?"

"What I *feel* is concerned," Tanya said, squinting. "Because the door's wide open."

Ellen froze. The front double doors, partly obscured by the portico and the railing along the porch, were both pushed in, exposing the dark entryway.

Ellen reached instinctively for her phone. "I thought you said no one had the key yet."

"I did," Sue confirmed. "But this is Missouri. People leave their doors open."

"To nature?" Ellen gestured to the forest edging the estate. "That's a coyote invitation."

"Oh, come on," Sue said, heading toward the front porch.

"Are we really going in there?" Tanya asked. "What if there are vagrants inside?"

"Or worse?" Ellen added with a frown.

"How did I end up with two scaredy cats for best friends?" Sue climbed the steps up to the porch, which wrapped around the west side of the house.

Tanya shook her head. "I say we wait for tomorrow's appointment with the real estate agent. This is crazy."

"We can check into the condo in thirty minutes," Ellen, who was looking at the time on her phone, pointed out. "If we go now, I bet they'd let us check in early."

Sue ignored them and stepped through the front door. "Let's just peek. One quick walkthrough. And don't worry. I've got my gun."

"That makes me feel better," Tanya muttered sarcastically.

The floorboards creaked ominously as Sue reached inside, flipping a switch on the wall. Nothing happened.

"Power's not on yet," Sue said, disappearing into the shadows. "Very atmospheric!"

Tanya made a sound that could only be described as a whimper. Ellen followed reluctantly, phone flashlight on and in hand, and Tanya brought up the rear, clutching her oversized tote like it was body armor.

The house smelled like dust, mothballs, and something less definable—wet dog mixed with attic—as they stepped into a large hall that was open to the second floor, with the staircase to their left and a Victorian fireplace to their right. A draft rattled against the grate on the hearth, sending chills up Ellen's spine.

"I thought the last owners were having this place professionally cleaned," Sue muttered.

"Maybe they did," Ellen began, "back in the eighties, when they last updated the décor." The wallpaper reminded her of the garden home she bought with Paul when they were first married. Then, she quickly added, "It's got great bones, though. Lots of Victorian charm."

Ellen could see a room with a second fireplace just off the entryway to the right as they continued walking toward the back and into a large living room.

"I'm going to enjoy ripping down that wallpaper," Tanya said. "I bet they named that design 'Eyesore.'"

"I like it," Sue insisted. "I'm thinking about keeping it."

Ellen huffed, knowing a joke when she heard one. She noticed the porch through a set of French doors to the west, and a dining room with yet another fireplace to the east. "This house has more fireplaces than a chimney sweeper's nightmare."

A noise echoed from the kitchen at the back of the house.

A scraping. A thump.

Tanya froze. "What was that?"

Sue whispered, "A ghost?"

Ellen frowned. "More likely a squirrel."

"Or a bear," Tanya hissed.

"Could be a black bear," Ellen said, sweeping her light across a second set of stairs separating the dining room from the kitchen. She crept forward. "Be ready to run."

"You don't run from black bears," Tanya reminded her. "Remember our dance in Hot Springs?"

"Great," Ellen sighed as she entered the kitchen and shined her light on the cabinets. "I didn't know I needed my dancing shoes today."

Sue tiptoed toward the pantry with her gun out, as if she were the leader of a S.W.A.T. team.

Ellen felt delirious as the adrenaline pumped through her.

Then it happened.

A shape burst from the pantry with a hissing screech, flinging itself into the air with limbs outstretched like a furry ninja. Tanya, who stood behind Sue, shrieked and swung her tote bag at it in pure primal instinct, knocking the creature to the floor.

The raccoon skidded and darted past Ellen's boots, through the house, and out the front door, its ringed tail a blur.

Ellen patted her chest and caught her breath. "That was exciting."

Tanya panted, holding her tote like a weapon. "It tried to kill me."

"It tried to escape," Ellen said. "From us."

"Did you get that on video?" Sue asked, patting her lashes to make sure they were still intact. "I want Tom to see what a badass I am."

"No," Ellen said. "But I'll write about your bravery in your obituary, right after I kill you."

Tanya adjusted her ponytail, chest still heaving. "Why'd it come after *me?* Sue was the one with the gun."

Sue grinned. "There's your answer, Sherlock."

Ellen shook her head, stepping onto the back porch for fresh air. The cold hit her like a blessing. She took a deep breath and looked out over the woods below. "What a lovely view," she called to the others.

Her friends joined her on the back porch to gaze down the hillside at the woods. On the horizon, the sun was just beginning its afternoon descent.

"I bet there are deer in there," Sue said of the woods as she stepped to the porch rail between Tanya and Ellen. "Tom and I could put a feeder right there and watch them from the living room."

"For now, watch for splinters," Tanya warned.

"Yeah, this needs to be sanded and repainted," Sue said of the rail.

As Ellen gazed down into the thick woods below, she thought she saw something moving in the trees. It was too tall to be a deer.

"Can we go now?" she asked.

"I want to take a quick peek at the upstairs," Sue persisted.

"Since when have you ever been excited about going up stairs?" Tanya chided.

"Wait in the car if you want. You can't blame me for being excited to see the place."

"We aren't letting you go up there alone," Ellen groaned with resignation.

"Speak for yourself," Tanya said. Then she added, "Look, there's a powder room beneath the stairs."

Sue poked her head into the doorway, where Tanya was standing. "Oh, yes. I may keep this room as is."

Ellen glanced inside from behind Sue, noticing the pedestal sink, round, antique mirror, and toilet. "I'm surprised there's no wallpaper in there."

Tanya, who had moved out of the way so the others could see the powder room, said, "Let's get this over with. It stinks in here. Which stairs? Front or back?"

Sue shrugged. "We may as well take these, since they're right here."

As Ellen followed Sue, she asked, "How far away are the Murder Caves?"

"They're actually called Murder Rocks," Sue corrected. "I've been calling them by the wrong name all these months, but the real estate agent corrected me yesterday. She's going to show them to us tomorrow. She said it's quite a hike, so wear walking shoes."

"I'm always up for a hike," Tanya put in from the rear.

"Show off," Sue complained.

"How's the research going on the treasure hunt?" Ellen asked Sue as they turned at the landing.

"I've got a lot of promising leads," Sue replied. Then she pinched her nose. "The smell gets worse up here."

"Smells like a dead animal," Tanya said.

As she reached the landing, Ellen heard Sue gasp from one of the bedrooms.

"Everything okay?" Ellen called as she caught up to her.

Sue stood just inside the room, still as a statue, staring at the floor. Sprawled near a broken window was a young man, mid-forties, lying in a pool of his own blood. He had short, brown hair and a baby-smooth face and was wearing a plaid shirt and blue jeans. He might have seemed like he was sleeping if his blue eyes weren't wide open and his plaid shirt wasn't soaked with blood. He lay on his back with a shard of the broken windowpane embedded in his chest.

Trembling, Ellen reached for her phone.

"I think I'm going to be sick," Tanya, clutching her stomach, moaned.

"Should I call 9-1-1?" Ellen wondered.

"The one who finds the body is always the prime suspect," Sue murmured, still holding her gun.

"I need to get out of here," Tanya said from the doorway before rushing down the stairs.

Sue backed away from the body and was about to follow Tanya but noticed she had blood on the bottom of her boots and was leaving prints on the wooden floor. "Oh, no."

Tapping her phone, Ellen said, "The universe is telling us what we should do. Calling is the right thing. Let's go downstairs to wait for the police."

The flashing red and blue lights sliced through the thickening dusk like neon blades. Ellen watched them from the bottom of the gravel driveway, arms wrapped around herself, the cold finally settling in her bones now that the adrenaline had begun to fade. Tanya sat silently in the front passenger's seat of their rental car, her knees drawn up, arms hugging her legs. Sue paced nearby in measured circles, glancing now and then at the blood still visible on her boots.

A Taney County sheriff's vehicle rolled to a stop, followed by a second cruiser. Two deputies exited the first, both men in khaki uniforms and wide-brimmed hats. The younger of the two looked barely out of college, his face still marred by the occasional breakout. The older one moved with the caution of a man who'd seen more than one body in a vacant house.

"You the ones who called?" the older deputy asked, stepping closer.

Ellen nodded and stepped forward. "Yes. I'm Ellen. This is Sue. Tanya's in the car."

"I'm Deputy Colton, this here's Deputy Reese," the man said. "Anyone else inside?"

"No," Sue replied. "Just the body."

Colton's gaze narrowed. "And how did you come upon it?"

"We were touring the house," Ellen said carefully. "My friend Sue just bought it. The door was open, and we thought we'd take a look."

Colton eyed them in turn. "So, no forced entry?"

"It didn't look like it," Ellen said. "But I didn't inspect the lock or anything."

"Did you touch anything?" Reese asked.

"I stepped in blood," Sue said, lifting her boot sheepishly. "Sorry."

Reese pulled a small notepad from his pocket and began scribbling.

"We didn't touch the body," Ellen added. "And I called as soon as we found it." She decided not to mention her moment of hesitation.

"We'll need to have a look," Colton said. "You ladies wait here."

As the deputies entered the house, followed by two more officers from the cruiser, Ellen returned to the rental car and opened the front passenger's door. "You doing okay?"

Tanya nodded numbly. "I just keep seeing his face. His eyes."

Ellen reached in and squeezed her arm. "It's going to be all right."

A few minutes passed before Deputy Reese reemerged, his expression grim. "Found an ID on him, along with this." He unfolded a piece of paper with gloved hands and held it out for them to inspect. "That mean anything to you?"

Ellen and Sue bent over the document.

"It's a map of Murder Rocks," Sue said. "Maybe he was looking for the treasure."

Reese turned to Colton. "Murder Rocks?"

"Folklore," the older deputy replied gruffly. "We've had our fair share of tourists injured while hunting for the lost gold, but this is the first murder."

"Murder?" Ellen's eyes widened. "You don't think it was an accident?"

"Still early days," Colton replied. Then, he added, "We've called in the coroner and will know more after she takes a look. Meanwhile, we'll need statements from each of you. Have you ever seen this man before? Name's Jason Albright."

Tanya and Ellen shook their heads.

"No, sir," Sue said. "And I was told the property would be empty until our walkthrough tomorrow."

"Your real estate agent—gotta name?" Colton asked.

"Kimberly Watkins."

Reese jotted it down. "We'll contact her. Might have to postpone your walkthrough until after the crime scene has been properly processed."

Colton handed Ellen his card. "Call me if you remember anything else."

Another cruiser arrived, this time with the coroner's van behind it. As the professionals filed into the house, Ellen found herself drifting to the edge of the woods, drawn to the same spot she'd gazed at earlier.

Something had been out there. Could it have been the murderer? Realizing she should have mentioned it to the officers, she ran back into the house and called, "Deputy?"

Colton looked down at her from the top of the front staircase. "Yeah?"

"I saw something out in the woods. I thought it might be a bear, but now . . . I don't know."

"I'll have some officers check it out. Call me if you think of anything else."

"Yes, sir." Ellen left the house and met Sue on the front porch.

"You thinking what I'm thinking?" Sue asked.

"That we've just walked into trouble?" Ellen replied with a laugh.

Sue gave a small, tight smile. "That it's a good thing we brought our equipment. Maybe a ghost or two can tell us what happened."

Behind them, Tanya groaned from the car. "Can we *please* go to the condo now?"

"For once," Ellen muttered, "I agree with Tanya."

Sue sighed. "Fine. But tomorrow, we're getting answers. And also bleach. Lots of bleach."

CHAPTER TWO

YouTube Clues

By the time they arrived at the condo, the sky had turned navy, and the first stars blinked through the thinning clouds. Branson below looked like a snow globe had exploded, every building strung with shimmering lights, the streets dotted with giant candy canes and lit-up reindeer. Ellen paused just inside the door of the two-bedroom rental, breathing in the scent of cinnamon pinecones and new carpet.

"Not bad," Sue said, wheeling her suitcase into the entryway. "Nice view. Cozy fireplace. No dead bodies."

"Please don't make that our standard," Tanya muttered as she pulled her bag behind her and headed to the bedrooms. "I need a shower. And therapy. Maybe a lobotomy."

"I'm claiming the master," Sue called.

"Wait, you got the master last time," Tanya protested.

"And the time before that," Ellen added.

Sue crossed her arms. "I also booked the condo and bought a murder house. That's worth some perks."

Ellen grinned. "Tanya, take the master. I'll bunk with Sue. I brought my earplugs and noisemaker, so I'll be fine."

Sue smirked. "That's what *you* think."

They dragged their bags into their respective rooms, and twenty minutes later, all three were changed into pajamas and sitting on the sofa with mugs of hot tea, blankets wrapped around their shoulders. Outside the balcony window, Branson sparkled like a holiday card come to life.

Sue opened her laptop and set it on the coffee table. "Okay, let's see what we can find on Jason Albright."

Tanya cringed. "Are we sure we want to do this tonight? I'm still trying to unsee his face."

"We might learn something important," Ellen argued. "It could help the police."

After a quick search, Sue clicked on a YouTube channel titled *Ozark Gold Hunter*. The banner featured a younger Jason posing in front of a map with a shovel over his shoulder. His most recent video had been broadcasted live that morning and was titled: "Murder Rocks: Tenth Time's a Charm."

Sue clicked play.

Jason's face filled the screen. "Hey everyone, Jason here, broadcasting live from the mouth of Murder Rocks. I've been chasing Alf Bolin's treasure for six years now, and I think I'm closer than ever. Let's go take a look."

The camera wobbled as he turned, revealing the jagged rock formation they'd heard so much about. Jason's voice carried excitement and a tinge of paranoia.

"For those new to the channel," he said, "Alf Bolin was a Civil War bushwhacker who supposedly hid a fortune in gold, silver, and supplies in these caves. There've been rumors of a curse ever since. Some say he's still protecting the stash from beyond the grave."

"Oh great," Tanya said, pulling the blanket more tightly around her. "A cursed treasure. That's exactly what we need."

"Wait," Ellen pointed to the screen. "Aren't those the clothes we found him in?"

"Oh, my God." Tanya covered her mouth.

"Shhh," Sue said. "Listen."

In the video, Jason paused. "Wait. Did you hear that?"

The three women leaned closer.

"It sounded like a kid," Jason whispered. "A boy. Hold on."

He stepped away from the cave entrance, swinging his flashlight toward the woods. The early morning sun glinted down through the leaves.

"Hey!" he shouted. "You okay out there?"

Jason paused, as though he heard something, but the camera didn't pick it up.

"I should call someone," Jason muttered. "But what if it's nothing? Did you guys hear it? Leave me a comment below."

"I don't hear anything, do you?" Tanya leaned forward.

"Listen—there it is again," he said, pointing the camera toward the trees.

"No," Sue replied as Ellen shook her head.

The next clip showed Jason trudging uphill through thick brush, his boots crunching over dead leaves.

"It's getting closer," he panted. "That voice. It's coming from that house."

Ellen's stomach flipped. On screen, Jason pointed his camera at the back of a now-familiar silhouette—a two-story Victorian with a wide porch, a turret, and three chimneys.

"My house," Sue whispered.

Jason stepped onto the back porch and peeked into a window. "Hello?" To the camera, he said, "Did you hear that? Sounds like it's coming from upstairs."

He followed the porch to the front of the house and approached the door, which swung open at his knock.

"Hello?" he called. "Is someone in here? Are you hurt?"

The interior was dark on camera, Jason's flashlight beam bouncing wildly as he stepped inside.

"There it is again," he said, walking toward the front staircase.

Ellen could feel her pulse picking up. "This is it," she murmured. "This is when it happened."

They watched as Jason ascended the stairs.

"I don't know what this place is," he said, "but it feels . . . wrong."

He reached the top, plodded down the hallway, and glanced in three of the four bedrooms before entering the fourth at the back of the house.

His expression changed instantly—from curiosity to confusion, then to horror.

"What the hell—" he began.

A shriek.

The camera fell, landing sideways. It showed Jason's feet twisting as he dropped to the floor, then cut to black.

All three women sat frozen.

"I think I'm going to be sick again," Tanya whispered.

"We need to call Deputy Colton," Ellen said, already reaching for her phone. "Did he give me a card?"

Sue pointed to the kitchen counter. "You left it there when we came in."

Ellen retrieved it and dialed.

Colton answered on the third ring. "Colton."

"Hi, this is Ellen McManius from earlier, at Murder Ranch. We just found something."

"You okay?"

"Yes, but we found Jason Albright's YouTube channel. His last video . . . it shows him going into the house, Sue's house, just before he died, which, according to his live broadcast, was this morning."

There was a pause. "What exactly does it show?"

"He hears a child's voice in the woods, follows it up to the house. Goes inside, goes upstairs, and . . . we see his reaction right before he dies."

"Text me the link," Colton said. "We'll take a look."

"Did your men find anything in the woods?" Ellen asked.

"Nothing yet. We've cleared the area, but we'll take another pass in the morning."

"And Kimberly Watkins?" Ellen added. "Any word?"

"We reached her. She's supposed to contact you to reschedule the walkthrough."

"Okay. Thank you. And Deputy? Would you mind keeping us in the loop?"

"Will do," he said. "And Ellen? Try to get some rest tonight."

"Right."

Ellen ended the call.

"Well?" Sue asked.

"They're going to watch the video and follow up. I need to text him the link. Can you email it to me from your laptop?"

Sue got to work. After a minute, Ellen copied and pasted the link from the email and sent it to the deputy. "There. I hope that helps."

"Good," Sue said. "Because I've made up my mind."

Tanya groaned. "I don't like the sound of that."

"But first, why did you ask about the woods, Ellen?" Sue suddenly asked.

Ellen hesitated. "I, I saw something out there. It was bigger than a deer. Probably a bear."

"Well, like I said, I've made up my mind. We're going back tomorrow night," Sue insisted. "If the cops are gone, we'll do our own investigation."

"No way," Tanya said. "Not unless we go to a show first. Something with sparkles and jazz hands."

Sue grinned. "Deal. One show, one séance."

"Do you think other treasure hunters might have killed him?" Ellen wondered. "Or maybe the ghost of Alf Bolin did it."

"Ghosts rarely have that kind of power," Tanya pointed out. "Maybe a vengeful spirit?"

Sue's phone buzzed. "It's Kimberly Watkins," she said just before she answered.

Ellen and Tanya watched as Sue recounted to Kimberly how they'd found the body. She then made plans to meet at Murder Ranch on Wednesday morning. That was in two days.

Sue hung up. "Kimberly confirmed that the cops said they'd be out of there by tomorrow evening." She turned to Tanya. "Better pick out a matinée."

Ellen looked out the window at the glittering town below. Something told her they weren't just chasing a legend anymore. They were walking straight into it.

Ellen stepped out onto the balcony of their condo, letting the sliding door thump shut behind her. The cool night air rushed into her face, clearing away the lingering scent of chamomile and peppermint from the tea Tanya had brewed. The lights of Branson sprawled out before her, a shimmering patchwork of reds, greens, and golds. Somewhere below, a distant saxophone was playing "Have Yourself a Merry Little Christmas," the melancholy notes rising faintly through the trees.

She wrapped the quilt more tightly around her and reached into her pocket for her phone.

Brian picked up on the second ring. "Hey, Sweetheart."

Ellen smiled. His voice was always a balm. "Hey. Sorry it's late."

"You kidding? I've been waiting for you to call. Everything all right? You sound weird."

She took a breath. "We, uh, had kind of a rough day."

Brian groaned. "What happened?"

Ellen leaned against the balcony railing. "We found a body."

"*What?*" Brian's voice jumped an octave. "What do you mean you found a body?"

"In an upstairs bedroom of Sue's new place."

"You're joking."

"I wish I were."

He exhaled sharply. "Are you okay?"

"I'm fine," she said, her voice calm but firm. "We all are. Just a little shaken."

"What happened? Was it a break-in? Was someone hurt?"

"Not us," she said. "The man was already dead when we found him. Looked like he'd fallen through a window. There was . . . a lot of blood."

"Jesus, Ellen." He paused. "You called the police, right?"

"Of course. They've been handling everything. The property's being treated as a crime scene—"

"A crime scene?" he echoed. "They think he was murdered?"

"They're considering it," she replied. "Needless to say, it will delay our renovations by a day or two."

"You just found a dead man, and you're still planning on moving forward like this is a home makeover show?"

Ellen laughed softly despite herself. "Welcome to Ghost Healers, Inc."

"I don't like it," Brian said. "What if there's a killer still hanging around?"

Ellen thought about the dark trees, the memory of the figure she'd seen—or imagined—lingering like a shadow at the back of her mind. "They didn't find anyone. And they're doing another sweep tomorrow, just to be safe."

There was silence on the other end.

She softened her voice. "I promise, if anything feels unsafe, we'll leave. But Sue's excited about the renovation. We'll take it slow."

He blew out a long breath. "Just promise me you won't go hunting for trouble."

Ellen hesitated, then offered the truth-adjacent version. "I promise we'll be careful."

"Hmph." Brian didn't sound entirely convinced. "Well, at least tell me something normal. How's the condo?"

"Beautiful," she said, turning to glance through the glass at the cozy living room inside, where Tanya had left a trail of slippers and tea mugs like breadcrumbs. "It smells like cinnamon and looks like a Christmas card. We're up on a hill, so the view is incredible."

"You deserve something nice after today," he said. "So do Sue and Tanya."

"They're already in bed," she said. "Tanya passed out before the tea was cold, and Sue started snoring thirty minutes ago."

"Lucky them."

Ellen smiled. "And how's Moseby?"

"Oh, you know. Moping around like he's the only one who got left behind. No protest poops in the house yet, but it's still early days."

Ellen laughed. "Put me on speaker."

There was a rustle, then Brian said, his voice distant, "Okay, he can hear you."

"Moseby?" Ellen cooed. "Hi, sweet boy. Mama loves you."

A sharp, muffled bark came through the line, followed by the click-clack of tiny claws on tile.

Brian laughed. "He just ran to the door and barked at it. Thinks you're about to walk in."

Her chest ached with love. "Tell him I'll be home before he knows it."

"I told him. He's unconvinced."

They were both quiet for a moment, each holding onto the silence like a thread between them.

"I miss you," Brian said.

"I miss you, too," she replied.

"Get some sleep, okay?"

"I will."

"Goodnight, El."

"Goodnight."

She ended the call and slipped the phone back into her pocket. The air had turned colder. The saxophone down the hill had fallen silent, replaced by the hush of winter wind moving through the pines.

As she gazed down at the holiday lights, she hoped, with every rational bone in her body, that what she'd seen earlier had been a bear.

Turning away, she slid the door open and crept back inside, careful not to wake Tanya, who had crashed in the master bedroom with the door open. Ellen tiptoed down the hall and into her own, where Sue lay sprawled beneath a pink-striped quilt, snoring like a chainsaw.

Ellen climbed into the twin bed across from her, turned off the lamp, turned on her noise machine, and stared at the ceiling.

The memory of the thing in the woods below Sue's house played on repeat in her mind. She pulled the covers around her shoulders and tried to think about Moseby's bark instead.

A Show and a Séance

The theater was opulent in a way that made Ellen feel underdressed, even in her "elevated" blazer and scarf combo. Red velvet curtains framed the grand stage, and sparkling chandeliers floated like constellations from the ceiling. The place was packed, every seat taken, but Ellen, Sue, and Tanya had lucked out with three prime spots in the front row.

"I've heard a lot of good things about this show," Sue whispered as she settled in.

"Magic makes me nervous," Ellen said, sinking into her seat. "Too much smoke and mirrors."

Ellen was about to say more when the house lights dimmed, and the orchestra launched into a pulse-pounding overture. Golden lights sparkled like stardust, and from behind a curtain stepped Rick Thomas himself—tall, sharp-jawed, and dressed like a Vegas ringmaster in a tailored black jacket with silver lapels.

"Look, he's wearing your blazer," Ellen teased Sue.

"Twinsies," Sue said with a laugh.

"Ladies and gentlemen," he boomed with a charismatic smile, "welcome to *The Mansion of Dreams,* where the impossible becomes possible, and the laws of physics politely excuse themselves for the evening."

The audience erupted in applause as Rick bowed deeply.

Ellen leaned forward, already captivated.

Rick began with smaller illusions—rings that linked and unlinked, silks that changed colors mid-air—but it was the birdcage trick that truly caught Ellen's attention.

A delicate golden birdcage sat on a pedestal at center stage. Inside was nothing—clearly empty. Rick lit a flame beneath it, the cage igniting in a whoosh of fire. The heat rippled visibly, and just as Ellen began to flinch, the flames twisted upward and transformed—instantly—into a live, white dove.

The audience gasped. Even Tanya's jaw dropped.

"He must've had a hidden compartment at the base of the cage," Ellen whispered, trying to sound confident. "Probably protected the dove from the fire, released it with some kind of spring."

Sue nodded thoughtfully. "Makes sense."

But then Rick tossed the dove gently into the air, and just as it flapped upward, its form shimmered, and what fluttered back down into Rick's waiting hand was no longer a dove but a folded white scarf.

Ellen blinked. "What?"

Rick held the scarf aloft. "The dreams don't stop until you wake up."

"How did he do that?" Ellen whispered, turning to her friends. "Did you see a trapdoor or something?"

Tanya shook her head, eyes wide. "That bird *disappeared*."

Sue just grinned. "Amazing."

But the next illusion proved even more baffling.

Rick gestured to center stage, where his assistants rolled out a large accordion-shaped box mounted on a simple wheeled platform. The table it rested on was no more than a flat wooden surface with visible legs and open space beneath—nothing enclosed, nothing hidden.

"I will now attempt the impossible," Rick announced, "with the help of my lovely assistant, Olivia."

Olivia, a graceful woman in a red evening gown, climbed the stairs at the side of the table and stepped into the accordion box. She crouched, knees to her chest, as Rick folded the top flaps shut.

"To eliminate all doubt," Rick continued, "you'll see the platform from every angle."

The second assistant, a tall woman in a sequined suit, spun the table slowly on its wheels. As it rotated, Ellen could clearly see under and around the platform. No traps. No hidden panels. Just open air beneath the table legs.

Olivia's hand appeared from one end of the box, fluttering her fingers toward the crowd. Rick placed a long-stemmed rose in it. The second assistant continued slowly spinning the table as Rick theatrically removed the rose and made it vanish into a puff of gold smoke.

Then, with great flourish, Rick climbed the stairs himself and approached the handle mounted on the side of the box.

"Now," he said, his voice low and dramatic, "we make her vanish."

He pushed the handle.

The accordion-shaped box collapsed flat like a crushed paper fan.

The audience gasped.

"Impossible," Ellen whispered, rising slightly in her seat. "Could she be inside the table somehow?"

"She'd be thinner than a yoga mat," Sue whispered back.

Just then, Rick turned toward the front row and met Ellen's eyes.

"You, madam," he said, extending a gloved hand. "Would you mind helping us out?"

Ellen looked behind her, sure he was pointing at someone else.

Rick smiled. "Yes, you—right there. With the tweed blazer and the curious eyes."

Sue elbowed her playfully. "Go on, Miss Skeptic."

Ellen rose to laughter and light applause, cheeks flushing as she made her way toward the stage stairs. Rick met her halfway and gallantly offered his hand.

"What's your name?" he asked.

"Ellen," she said, suddenly hyperaware of hundreds of eyes on her.

"Well, Ellen, I need you to verify that there's no trickery here—no trapdoors, no optical illusions."

He led her to the table. "Go ahead. Check underneath."

Ellen bent over and swept her hand beneath the platform, waving it between the legs and under the center.

"Just air," she confirmed.

"And now up the steps, please."

Oh, lord. She had to climb steps? In front of an audience? Praying her knees wouldn't give as they trembled nervously, she moved to the steps.

Rick held one hand while his assistant took the other, guiding Ellen to the top of the table. From this angle, the accordion box—now completely flattened—looked even more impossibly thin.

"Ready?" Rick asked.

"I think so," Ellen replied.

"Together now," he said, placing her hand on the handle. "Let's bring the dream back."

They pulled the lever, and the accordion structure re-expanded with a satisfying *whump*.

Rick and the assistant helped Ellen down as the audience buzzed with anticipation.

Then Rick broke open the sides of the box with a dramatic flourish.

Olivia was there—kneeling, smiling, and very much intact.

She rose to her feet, threw her arms up to wild applause, and beamed.

Ellen could only stare.

As Olivia stepped forward, Rick gestured to her. "A round of applause for Olivia!"

The crowd cheered.

"And for our volunteer, Ellen!"

The applause surged again as Ellen waved awkwardly, still too stunned to smile fully. The second assistant helped her off the stage and back to her seat.

Sue leaned over and whispered, "That'll teach you to keep your skepticism to yourself."

"I don't understand," Ellen muttered, sinking back into her chair. "There was nowhere to hide. I *checked*."

"Well," Tanya said, eyes still on the stage, "looks like we're not the only ones dabbling in the supernatural this week."

Ellen chuckled, despite herself.

And for the first time since finding the body at Sue's new house, her mind had been momentarily taken off the murder.

Momentarily.

Because even as the applause echoed around her, and Rick took his final bow, Ellen couldn't help but glance again beneath the illusionist's table.

Sunday evening, the sky over Branson had turned the color of blueberry cobbler as Ellen guided their rental Chevy Onix down JJ Highway. A sense of comfort clung to her like warm cinnamon, courtesy of the decadent dinner they'd just devoured. She could still taste Paula Deen's famous Gooey Butter Cake on her tongue—sweet, rich, and unapologetically Southern.

"I swear, if I die tomorrow, bury me in that butter cake," Sue said from the back seat, her voice dreamy with satisfaction.

"Me, too," Tanya agreed, cradling her stomach with a groan. "That was delicious, but so rich. I shouldn't have eaten so much."

"I couldn't help myself," Ellen admitted as she turned onto the gravel drive leading to Sue's newly purchased Victorian house.

Tanya straightened in her seat. "I don't see any crime scene tape."

"No police cruisers either," Ellen added, slowing to a crawl.

"Guess they're done processing the scene," Sue said, a strange note of anticipation in her voice. "Perfect."

Ellen parked beneath the tall oaks lining the front of the estate. The house loomed ahead, its silhouette skeletal against the moonlight. Every window was dark.

No welcome lights. No porch glow.

Just the kind of silence that carried a whisper of dread.

They retrieved their bags of paranormal gear from the trunk: cameras, EVP recorder, spirit box, sage bundle, candles, headlamps—the same tools they'd used at more than a dozen haunted properties. Normally, Ellen found the ritual comforting. But tonight, her hands trembled as she slung her SLS camera over her shoulder.

The woods were darker at night.

Inside, the house smelled faintly of dust and old wood. Now that the body was gone, the smell had improved. She wondered if there was a stain left behind on the second floor. She'd wait until daylight to return up there.

They gathered in the front room with the second fireplace, to the right of the entryway, where a wide hearth sat cold and empty.

"Here," Tanya said, sitting on the ledge beside it. She pulled three white pillar candles from her tote and arranged them in a triangle at the center of the stone.

Ellen and Sue sat on either side of her.

Tanya struck a match, lit the candles, and then used a small bundle of sage to smudge the circle, its pungent aroma filling the room in thin, snaking tendrils.

"For protection," she murmured.

Ellen adjusted her headlamp and switched on the SLS camera. A few flickers of static, then the grid appeared—lines crisscrossing the screen like digital spiderwebs.

Tanya slid on headphones and plugged them into the EVP recorder. Her eyes were wide, but her posture was steady as she held the microphone out, hoping to pick up the faintest of sounds.

Sue clutched the full-spectrum camera. "Okay," she said softly. "Here goes." She cleared her throat. "To any spirits who may be here, we mean you no harm. We come in peace, and with respect. Is anyone here with us tonight?"

For a long moment, there was only the soft crackle of the sage and the occasional shifting creak of the house settling.

Then—the leftmost candle flickered once . . . twice . . . and went out.

Tanya inhaled sharply.

Sue turned her camera toward the candles. "Was that you?" she asked gently. "If so, can you give us another sign?"

Ellen's eyes scanned her screen.

A figure—skeletal, stick-like, and unmistakably humanoid—materialized on the bottom step of the front staircase on the other side of the entryway from her. The landing of the staircase was near the turret, where moonlight shone in through its curved windows.

"There's something on the stairs," Ellen whispered. "Looks like a child. Small. Very small."

Sue leaned forward. "A little sprite?"

Tanya blinked. "Could it be the boy Jason said he heard in the woods? The one calling for help?"

Ellen didn't answer. Her focus was glued to the flickering stick-figure on her screen.

"Could that child have been the one who . . . killed Jason?" Sue asked aloud.

The other two candles snuffed out at once.

The room plunged into darkness, save for the pale beams of their headlamps and the little bit of moonlight sifting through the front windows.

A shiver danced across Ellen's spine. "Maybe it's not a child," she whispered, "but the twisted ghost of Alf Bolin."

She switched on the spirit box. It whirred to life, spitting static in irregular bursts.

She leaned toward the device, her voice steady. "Whoever you are, we'd like to know what happened here. What do you know about the death of Jason Albright?"

The figure on her SLS screen twitched. It turned—*moved*—toward the entryway.

"It's coming toward us," she whispered.

The chill deepened, settling in her bones.

Suddenly, Tanya yelped and sprang to her feet, ripping off her headphones.

"Something pulled my hair!"

Ellen's breath caught.

Sue raised her camera. "Was that you? Are you trying to communicate? Do you want us to leave?"

Through the spirit box, a single word crackled out—distorted but unmistakable:

"Yes."

Tanya's eyes widened. "Okay. That's it. I'm out. Message received."

Ellen frowned. "But why do you want us to leave?" she asked the air. "We're not here to hurt you."

On her screen, the stick-figure vanished.

She panned the room with the camera. Nothing. Gridlines. Empty space.

"I've lost it," she said. "It's not showing up anymore."

Before Sue could respond, Ellen felt it.

A *scratch*—sharp and sudden—just beneath the base of her neck, like claws, had dragged across her skin.

She jerked upright with a hiss. "Okay, *I'm* ready to go, too. I just got scratched."

Sue's expression changed. "You sure?"

Ellen turned and swept her hair aside. Tanya angled her headlamp.

"Three narrow red marks," Tanya confirmed. "I can see them clear as day at the base of her neck. Let's get out of here. This thing is aggressive." She began stuffing the extinguished candles into her tote with shaky hands. "I am *not* getting possessed tonight."

As they packed, Tanya said to Sue, "I thought you said the realtor told you there weren't any reports of hauntings."

"That's what Kimberly told me," Sue replied as she climbed to her feet.

"Maybe this sprite came from the woods," Ellen said, remembering the figure she had seen—though it had been larger than a child.

"Then maybe it should go back there," Sue said boldly, glancing once more toward the turret and staircase before heading out the front door.

They didn't speak again until they were in the car, doors shut, seatbelts on, engine running.

As Ellen turned the wheel and eased down the gravel drive, she exhaled a breath of relief.

From the back seat, Sue broke the silence.

"Before we begin renovations," she said, her voice soft but firm, "we're going to need to clean house . . ."

A beat passed.

". . . and I don't mean with a mop."

CHAPTER FOUR

The Official Tour

From the front porch of the Victorian, the view on Monday morning was breathtaking. Rolling hills blanketed in pine and oak sprawled toward the horizon. The mist still clung to the hollows, but sunlight filtered through in golden ribbons. Ellen leaned on the wooden railing, inhaling the crisp, pine-scented air as she gazed over their parked car toward the woods. To her right, the porch curved gracefully around the west side of the house and continued past a covered carport that had once served as a stagecoach stop. A decorative iron lantern hung from its ceiling, swaying slightly in the breeze. From there, the porch continued, wrapping around to the back of the house.

"Hard to believe this place was built in 1918," Kimberly Watkins said as she joined the women on the porch, tablet in hand. She wore a smart green blazer and had her chestnut hair clipped back, a pen tucked behind one ear. "It's one of the oldest surviving homes in the Pine Hill area."

"1918?" Sue echoed, gazing up at the tall front turret. "I would have guessed earlier."

"It has that look," Kimberly agreed. "But the land itself wasn't available for private ownership until 1899, after the U.S. government released it. William H. Johnson, a lawyer and early developer of Hollister, was one of the first to snatch it up. He never lived here, though—he flipped it to out-of-state investors, hoping to cash in on timber and mining. But the mines dried up fast, and the trees were already stripped for railroad ties."

"So, they gave up," Ellen said, arms crossed. "What about the people who built the house?"

"That would be Elmer Dean Jackson and his wife, Orpha," Kimberly replied. "He bought the land in 1918 and moved his family here to raise livestock. Elmer Dean was the first Jackson to own Murder Rocks, the land just behind the house."

Ellen exchanged a glance with Tanya and said, "We're looking forward to the hike today."

"It's got quite the reputation," Kimberly said with a small smile. "Elmer's son, Dean Hall Jackson, became a teacher and minister. In the 1930s, he wrote a beautiful article about the rocks. He described the limestone formations below the old Springfield-Harrison Road as 'inspiring,' surrounded by cedar and grapevines."

"Sounds poetic," Tanya murmured.

"He was," Kimberly said. "But even he couldn't deny the rumors. That place has a dark past—robberies, ambushes, even murder. Hence the name."

Sue perked up. "Shall we head there now? Or after the walkthrough?"

"Let me show you the house first," Kimberly said, waving her hand toward the front door. "As I mentioned to you before, Russell Jackson, the man who sold it to you, wanted Murder Rocks preserved. That's why he included a clause in the sale that the rocks would eventually be donated to the county to create a park with safer access."

"Too many treasure hunters getting hurt?" Ellen asked as she followed Sue inside.

"Exactly. Russell said people were constantly knocking on his door asking about the place—or trespassing outright. He figures a formal trail and signage will cut down on injuries *and* visitors."

"Well," Tanya said, entering the house after Ellen, "we better find that treasure before the county gets their hands on it."

Kimberly followed them through the double front doors, which swung open into a wide entryway with tall ceilings and gleaming wood floors. A chandelier overhead sent scattered light across the floral wallpaper.

"The power's on!" Sue cried with a huge grin.

"Turned on this morning," Kimberly explained. "The formal parlor is on your right," Kimberly added, pointing. "Notice the fireplace and original plaster medallions."

Ellen glanced at the stone hearth, where she and her friends had conducted their investigation the previous night.

"Love the bay window," Tanya murmured.

"Dining room's right through there," Kimberly pointed past the parlor toward the back of the house. "Big enough for a ten-top table. That door leads past the second staircase to the kitchen."

They wandered room to room, Ellen trailing her fingers along the intricate woodwork. The house was dated but solid, filled with light and the faint smell of lemon-scented cleaner.

"There's another room just here," Kimberly said, pointing through the cased opening that led to a large living area. It was located between the entry hall at the front of the house and the kitchen at the back. "Could be used as a second living area, a study, or a library."

"And Russell didn't mention anything to you about ghosts?" Sue asked.

"No, and I asked," Kimberly replied. "Though after what happened Saturday, I suppose anything's possible."

They made their way through the kitchen and to the back stairs.

"Russell added a powder room beneath these steps for convenience," Kimberly said. "Small, but functional."

"Thank goodness," Tanya muttered. "I'd hate to go upstairs every time I needed to go."

"Especially with your pea-sized bladder," Sue put in with a chuckle as she followed Kimberly through the dining room and parlor and back toward the front door.

"The view from the turret is a pretty one," Kimberly said at the base of the grand staircase that looked down over the large hall below.

"I'd turn that into a reading nook," Ellen suggested, pointing to the base of the turret, as Kimberly ascended the stairs.

"Good idea," Sue agreed before following in Kimberly's footsteps.

"This provides a pretty vantage point to the house downstairs," Kimberly added. "You can see how gorgeous that crystal chandelier is from here."

From the upstairs landing, Kimberly took them to the top of the turret, which revealed a pretty bathroom with amazing views. A lounge off the bath opened to a small balcony that overlooked the front of the property. They stepped out to have a look.

"What stunning views," Tanya remarked.

"Wait until you see the balcony off the master," Kimberly said as she re-entered the house. "But first, here's one of the secondary bedrooms. It has a bay window, like the parlor below it, with more gorgeous views to the south."

"Lovely," Ellen agreed. "This will be my room."

Sue snorted. "We'll see about that."

After viewing a small closet, they returned to the hall and to a second bedroom, adjacent to the first. It had east-facing windows with a different view of the woods below. The windows flanked a fireplace.

"The sunrise is gorgeous from here," Kimberly pointed out. "And this is the only bedroom with a fireplace."

"I'll take this room, thank you very much," Tanya cooed.

Sue shook her head and laughed. "As long as everyone agrees that the master is mine."

"Well, it is *your* house," Ellen said.

"Speaking of the master," Kimberly began, "it's right across the hall."

Ellen followed the others to the large room with its even larger balcony overlooking the west side of the property.

Kimberly opened the French doors and stepped outside. "Imagine watching the sunsets from here."

Ellen and her friends followed the real estate agent onto the balcony, which was covered by a portico with arches and rails. The balcony jutted out far and wide over the carport beneath it.

Ellen gazed out at the horizon and the woods below. "Stunning. What a great find, Sue. I couldn't be happier for you."

"You will be when we find that treasure," she said with a raised finger.

"Check out the *en suite*," Kimberly said as she led them back inside.

"It's huge," Tanya cried with disbelief. "I wouldn't expect this in such an old house."

"It was added much later," Kimberly explained. "It was originally another balcony."

"That explains its curved shape," Sue remarked. "I love it."

"That clawfoot tub is gorgeous," Kimberly pointed out, "and it overlooks the back of the estate."

"There's one more bedroom left to see," Sue said with a suddenly somber tone. "I'm afraid to go in there, to tell you the truth."

"Me, too," Tanya agreed.

"Don't be afraid," Kimberly said. "I had professional cleaners come early this morning. They cleaned the whole house and were able to get the blood stains from the floor."

"No wonder everything smells fresher today," Sue noted.

Ellen led the way into the room where they had discovered the body of Jason Albright. The room was bright now. The floors were clean. No blood. No signs of violence.

Ellen moved to the window, where the broken panes had been removed and a plastic covering had been taped around the opening.

"I have someone coming to install a new window tomorrow," Kimberly told them.

"This room doesn't have a closet," Sue noticed.

"It was originally used as a music room—a conservatory," Kimberly explained. "But in more recent decades, the Jacksons used it as a fourth bedroom, using an armoire to store clothing."

"Hmm, I can live with that," Sue said. "I see this as a bunk room for the grandchildren, and they won't need a closet, anyway."

Tanya glanced at Ellen, and Ellen could read her friend's mind: She wouldn't put grandchildren in the same room where the murder victim had been found.

Kimberly led them from the bedroom to the back staircase, which provided access to the attic. Although plenty of light filtered in through windows facing the north, east, and south, it was dusty and unfinished.

"Great storage up here," Kimberly remarked. "Or you could convert it into a bonus space—maybe another bedroom, bath, and game room."

"That's certainly something to think about," Sue said, considering.

"Is there a basement?" Tanya asked.

Kimberly shook her head. "Only a crawl space."

"So, this completes the tour?" Sue asked.

"All but the hike to Murder Rocks," Kimberly replied with a grin.

"Lead the way," Sue cried. "I'm probably more excited about the caves than I am the house!"

With flashlights in hand, Ellen, Sue, and Tanya followed Kimberly down the wooded slope behind the mansion. The trail was faint but visible, a narrow path lined with roots and moss-covered rocks. As they descended, the trees closed in.

"Watch your step," Kimberly said over her shoulder. "The trail isn't always clear."

"It's beautiful, though," Tanya said, panting a little as she picked her way down the slope. "Like something out of a fairytale."

"Maybe *Little Red Riding Hood*," Ellen muttered. "Or *Hansel and Gretel*." She kept her eye out for the figure she had seen, the figure she now hoped was not, in fact, a bear.

The woods opened slightly as they neared the base of the hill, revealing massive limestone formations jutting from the earth like pre-historic ruins.

"There they are," Kimberly said, gesturing with her flashlight. "Murder Rocks. Russell says the old Springfield-Harrison Road ran just above those boulders. All of that got buried when the new highway came through."

Ellen stared at the jagged stones. They loomed over them like ancient gods, their surfaces scarred and stained with time. The shadows between them looked deep enough to swallow a person whole.

"People still come here?" Tanya asked.

"All the time," Kimberly replied. "As I said, Russell used to get knocks on his door from tourists, ghost hunters, and treasure seekers. Some know the location and sneak in. Some ask permission. Some get hurt."

"Ghost hunters?" Sue asked. "Any paranormal activity reported out here?"

"Russell once told me that he's not superstitious, but he wouldn't camp here overnight."

Sue stepped closer to the rocks. "That's where Jason Albright shot his video."

"That's right," Ellen said, keeping her distance. "You can see the cave entrance up there."

Sue climbed a few feet up toward the opening.

"Be careful," Tanya called nervously. "You saw what happened to him."

"If you hurt yourself," Ellen warned, "we're rescheduling renovations. We're not doing them without you."

"Watch her do it on purpose," Tanya said. "Just to get out of work."

Sue laughed. "I'm hiring contractors for the heavy stuff. We're just doing the fun parts, remember?"

Ellen crossed her arms. "Define fun."

Sue paused at the cave entrance, shining her flashlight inside. "Creepy. But I get why Jason was intrigued. I can't wait to start hunting."

"For ghosts or treasure?" Kimberly asked.

"Both," Sue replied.

"Come back down, Indiana Jones," Ellen called.

Sue rejoined them a moment later, breathless but grinning. "Nothing inside but shadows and cobwebs. But the treasure is there, I can feel it."

They climbed back up the slope together, flashlight beams bouncing. The house glowed above them in the fading light.

At the top, Kimberly pulled the keys from her coat pocket and handed them to Sue. "Officially yours. Good luck."

"Thanks," Sue said, accepting them with a grin. "We'll need it." Then, turning to her friends, she asked, "Ready to help me with the kitchen cabinet measurements?"

CHAPTER FIVE

Let the Renovations Begin

The morning light made the wraparound porch glow like a ring of honey as Ellen pulled their rental onto the gravel drive. Frost clung to the grass, glittering in the hollows between juniper clumps. The air held that bright, brittle cold that promised a clear day if you were brave enough to step into it. She cut the engine and listened to the gravel settle, the birds chirping, distant traffic on JJ, and a woodpecker somewhere down the ridge—everything else was still.

A pickup with a ladder rack waited near the porch steps. A man in a canvas jacket and a ball cap pushed his hands deeper into his pockets as they climbed out of the SUV. He had the compact build of someone who lifted cabinets for fun and the steady gaze of someone who preferred things level and square.

"You must be Sue," he said, tipping his head toward her. "Caleb Rivera. Rivera Restoration & Remodel." His eyes slid to Ellen and Tanya, kind but appraising the way contractors always were, as if measuring who would ask for the impossible. "I'm surprised you already hired somebody else. I could have met you yesterday, as originally planned."

Sue paused, a hand halfway extended. "Come again?"

Caleb hooked a thumb toward the side of the house. "Guy in a van pulled in about twenty minutes ago. Said he was here to install a window. Figured you'd found yourself another contractor."

"Oh!" Ellen's breath clouded in the air as understanding clicked. "Kimberly—the real estate agent—hired a window guy to replace the broken pane. Not a remodeler."

Caleb's mouth tugged at one corner. "That makes more sense. I thought I'd lost the job before I'd even shaken hands."

"We're all yours," Sue said, recovering her smile. "You come highly recommended by Ellen's husband, Brian—Brian McManius."

"Brian's a good man," he said.

Ellen smiled with pride and felt a tinge of homesickness as she followed the others toward the house.

They moved toward the porch, boots crunching gravel. Up close, the Victorian's trim wore decades of sun like crow's feet around a laughing eye—endearing from a distance, flaking up close. The porch wrapped from the front to the west flank of the house and continued beneath the covered carport—the old stagecoach cover—its posts stout and square, decorative brackets scalloped with a scroll saw's imagination. Ellen loved the proportions of it: wide enough for wicker chairs and a generous runner of ferns; high enough to lift you above the slope and hang you in the air.

"Exterior paint," Sue said, a decisive little clap of her hands. "I'd like to keep the original trim and repair rot where needed, but we're refreshing the color."

Caleb ran a thumb along a flake and tilted it in the light. "Lead-safe practices, containment, full scrape within reason and sand, epoxy patch, then a bonding primer. We'll rope and harness on the second story. You got colors yet?"

"Soon," Sue said. "I'm leaning blue and gray, but we still have to shop."

"Front doors?" he asked, nodding at the double slabs, handsome even under the dullness—their panels were raised and their glass lights bevel-cut like little prisms.

"Sanded and stained," Sue said. "Not painted."

Caleb jotted notes on a clipboard. "We'll mask the glass and put new weather strip on the jambs. Might replace the sweeps."

He stepped back to view the fascia running to the carport. "I'd like to sister that far left joist under the porch edge—you see that sway? We'll tuck a steel bracket and lag them in from below. It'll stiffen the bounce."

"Please do," Ellen said. The phantom sensation of last night's scratch stirred at the base of her neck, and she pushed her scarf higher without thinking.

Inside, the foyer breathed lemon and old wood.

"The floors," Tanya said, bending to touch the grain, "they're gorgeous."

"Previous owner did you a favor," Caleb said, crouching to check the transition. "Nice refinish. I don't recommend another pass unless you want a different stain. These will last if you cover high traffic during work."

"We'll baby them," Sue said. "Okay—interior paint. We can do the wallpaper removal and a lot of the painting ourselves—"

"*We?*" Tanya murmured.

"—but I want two estimates: one with you doing wallpaper removal and interior paint, and one without. We're still negotiating how much sweat equity is . . . fun."

"I'll break down labor and materials for both," Caleb said.

They moved through the pocket doors into the dining room. The windows had a delicate arch at the top, filled with wavy glass that distorted the woods beyond into painted strokes. Ellen loved that about old windows: when you looked through them, you were looking through history.

"The fireplaces stay as they are," Sue said. "They're perfect."

"Operational?" he asked.

"According to the inspection."

"Copy that."

The kitchen, at the rear of the house, wore its age without apology. The cabinets were units from the seventies with printed woodgrain and thin doors. The countertop might have been laminate in a past life and now was . . . laminate in decline. A frilly valance drooped over the sink, which looked out toward the woods.

"Kitchen's a complete gut," Sue said, lighting up in a way that made Ellen both proud and nervous. "We want to reconfigure the footprint. Refrigerator goes here, on this wall, with a proper cabinet enclosure. The stove moves opposite, where it can vent to the exterior, and the sink stays put—you've got your main line and a good view. Also, shaker-style cabinets. Probably gray. Here are the measurements I took for the cabinet layout I want."

Caleb took the paper from Sue. "Island where?"

"Centered, parallel with the sink wall," Sue said, walking the rectangle with her hands. "Seating for four, drawers on the cook side, trash pull-out on the end. We'll add a second prep sink if there's room."

"You'll want to mind clearances with those back stairs," he said, glancing over to the switchback that rose to the second floor. "But we can give you a good flow. Any appliances specified?"

"Not yet," Ellen said. "We'll shop after lunch. We grabbed granite samples already."

"Pull electric to code," Caleb said, ticking through an invisible list. "Dedicated circuits for appliances, GFCIs near sink, new supply lines, shut-off valves. What about the powder room under the stairs?"

"Keep as is," Sue said.

Ellen thought of the tiny room and its tucked-away privacy, the way it pressed against the underbelly of the stairs like a secret. She felt a little protective of it. Not everything needs to be new to be worthy, she thought.

They climbed the back stairs—narrow but charming—emerging at the second-floor landing. Sue led the group through the primary bedroom through to the primary bath.

"Let's keep the footprint," Sue said. "Gut the rest. The clawfoot stays and gets refinished—inside and out. Add a double-sink vanity along that straight wall, granite top, pretty backsplash. All new tile on the floor."

Caleb nodded, testing the subfloor with a toe tap. "We'll add cement board underlayment. Tile your floor, retile tub surround, or you keeping exposed cast iron?"

"Exposed tub," Sue said. "The surround can be wainscoting and paint."

While they spoke, Ellen drifted toward the north-facing window. The woods dropped away here; the grade steepened quickly, and then softened into a tangle of cedar and oak. She didn't want to find anything among the trees, and she didn't. No large shape lingering between trunks. No figure bigger than a deer. Just the occasional bird.

She exhaled, nice and slow, a sense of calm washing over her.

Sue led them out onto the large balcony off the master suite, which overlooked the west and would surely show stunning sunsets in the future.

"This railing needs to be sanded and repainted," Sue pointed out to Caleb, "and the decking may need to be stained, too."

"Got it," Caleb said as he made a note.

Someone rapped lightly on the balcony door before opening it and waving. "Howdy." A man in a blue company polo leaned through the doorway. Another man stood behind him, balancing a new sash in gloved hands.

"We're just finishing up," the first said. "New glass is in. We'll caulk and be out of your hair in twenty minutes."

"Thank you," Sue said with a wave.

The two men waved again and returned to their work.

Ellen and the others didn't follow the workers into the room. None of them suggested it. The scent of fresh caulk drifted down the hall anyway, mingled with lemon cleaner and a memory Ellen tried not to think about.

They crossed the master bedroom and headed for the turret. The turret bath sat like a jewel in the southwest corner, its curved wall holding a clawfoot tub like a ship in a rounded bay. Light made the room glow, and Ellen could see how, with care, it could become the sort of place where steam and eucalyptus solved problems.

"Same song," Sue said. "Keep the layout. Gut. Vanity with two sinks if they'll fit. Retile the shower, floor to ceiling. New glass door. Tile the floor. Resurface clawfoot with no surround."

"Noted." Caleb checked the ceiling height and the vent. "We'll run a new fan with a humidity sensor."

Caleb led them toward the main staircase at the front of the house. Sun pooled like warm milk on the landing, gilding the banister. The rail had been recently refinished; its sheen caught the light without shouting, and the newel post stood stately, a turned cap smooth enough to invite a palm.

"I wouldn't change a thing here," Sue said. "It's perfect."

Caleb ran a hand along the rail. "You can feel the craftsmanship in this piece. We'll tape it off and protect it during work."

Back in the foyer, they discussed timing and order. Caleb laid out a sequence—demo, supplies, installations, inspections, finishes—and promised to email two estimates by end of day: one with wallpaper removal and interior paint, one without. He would break out the kitchen, each upstairs bath, exterior paint, and porch repairs as separate line items, too.

As Caleb climbed into his truck, Sue stood with Ellen and Tanya on the porch, arms folded against the crisp air.

"Ready to clean house?" Sue asked, bouncing on her toes.

Tanya turned a shade paler. "Can we eat first? I feel faint."

"That's the first sign of a demon attachment," Ellen said, half-teasing.

Tanya cut her a look. "Don't joke about that."

"Mel's Hard Luck Diner," Sue announced, cheerful as a radio jingle. "Servers who sing and milkshakes thick enough to stand a spoon in. Come on."

They watched Caleb's truck bump down the drive. The house seemed to settle around them, stretching quietly in the cold. Ellen rubbed her scarf against the spot on her neck where last night's scratches had faded to thin pink lines. She imagined the house hearing the word *demolition* and bracing itself.

"We'll take care of you," she whispered, more to the wood than to her friends.

"Who are you talking to?" Tanya asked.

"Old wood," Ellen said, poker-faced. "It responds to reassurance."

They laughed, and the three of them clattered down the steps and into the day.

Mel's Hard Luck Diner welcomed Ellen and her friends with the scent of hot griddle and toasted buns and a chorus of doo-wop harmonies. The décor was unapologetically fifties: checkerboard tile, chrome-edged tables, and vinyl booths the color of maraschino cherries. A jukebox glowed against the far wall like a spaceship.

"Welcome to Mel's!" called a blond young man with eyes as blue as a new swimming pool. He wore a crisp white shirt and a midnight bow tie that matched his apron. "Sit wherever you like, ladies!"

They slid into a booth by the window, parking their handbags onto the bench along with fan decks of paint swatches, a hardbound book of granite slabs, and a binder of cabinet profiles. Tanya groaned the way people do when plopped between hunger and homework.

"Food first," she said, picking up a menu like it weighed several pounds.

"Order while your blood sugar still allows you to be kind," Ellen said.

Their server—Mr. Swimming Pool Eyes—appeared with water glasses that caught the neon and made it glitter. His name tag read "Bradley."

"What can I get you to start?" he asked in a baritone already warmed up.

"Coffee," Ellen said. "And maybe a milkshake to share."

"Chocolate," Tanya said. "Please. And fries."

"I'll be right back with that, unless you're ready to order," Bradley said.

"We're ready," Tanya said—or, pleaded, to be precise.

"Burger," Ellen said. "Medium with all the veggies. No cheese, please."

"Patty melt for me," Tanya said.

"Chicken-fried steak," Sue said brightly. "White gravy. And I'd love to hear you sing later."

Bradley winked. "Darlin', I'm happy to oblige." He collected menus and dashed away.

When he left, the three of them fell on the sample books like raccoons on a campsite.

"Exterior first," Sue said, laying out two big fan decks. "I want gray with blue trim. Not baby blue—royal or navy. And a fresh white for accents."

Ellen fanned swatches like a hand of cards. "Are we leaning warm or cool?"

"Cool," Sue said, tapping a crisp, modern slate. "We have a lot of green around the house—the woods will keep it from going too cold."

"Trim?" Tanya asked, flipping to a royal that verged on navy.

"That one," Sue said, almost instantly.

Ellen lined up the trio on the table: Slate Gray body, Royal Blue trim, Crisp White accents. "Beautiful. I like it."

"Me, too," Tanya said with a nod.

"Interior," Ellen said, flipping to a calm spectrum. "You said reverse inside: blue walls, gray trim."

"Right," Sue said. "A softer blue for living spaces, moodier blue for the dining room and parlor maybe, with gray casings and baseboards to keep it grounded."

Bradley returned with coffee mugs and a milkshake wearing a crown of whipped cream so tall it defied building codes. He set down a basket of fries whose aroma nearly made Ellen forgive every bad decision she'd ever made.

"Bless you," Tanya said, reaching for a fry like it had healing powers.

While they ate, Sue opened the granite book to a spread of stone that glittered with mica. "Kitchen surfaces. I want gray cabinets, and a slab with gray, white, and blue veining—something to tie the palette together without looking like toothpaste."

Ellen paged through options. "This one," she said, tapping a photo labeled Azul Platina—white ground, stormy gray rivers, occasional threads of blue, like veins of sea. The effect was lively without screaming.

"Yes," Sue said. "And brushed nickel or chrome for hard-ware—very clean."

"Oiled bronze," Ellen said, not missing a beat. "It'll pop against gray. Chrome will blend too much. Bronze gives you contrast and a nod to age."

"Gold," Tanya said through a fry. "Hear me out. Not gaudy eighties' brass—unlacquered brass. It would warm up the gray and tie to the Victorian fireplaces."

"Brass trends scare me," Sue said. "It's a bit trendy right now, isn't it? Might be outdated before we know it."

"It's not a trend if it's historically consistent," Ellen said. "And gold would be pretty, though I still favor oiled bronze for contrast."

"Chrome is easiest to source," Sue countered.

"You need to make a decision," Tanya said, gesturing with a fry like a judge's gavel.

Bradley reappeared with plates that made the table groan happily. Ellen's burger shone with a buttered bun, the patty seared dark at the edges like it had been kissed by a very affectionate grill. Sue's chicken-fried steak wore gravy like a bespoke coat. Tanya's patty melt oozed cheese in a way that would have deeply offended a cardiologist.

Conversation paused while they ate. For a few blessed minutes there were only little noises—the crunch of a fry, the sigh that follows a perfect first bite, the muffled hum of a neighboring booth where a small child tried to drink a milkshake faster than physics allowed.

"So," Sue said at last, licking a thumb and flipping a page with it, "exterior: gray, royal blue trim, white accents. Interior: blue walls, gray trim. Kitchen: gray cabinets, Azul Platina counters. Hardware: let me sleep on chrome versus bronze versus brass."

"You have until the estimates land," Ellen said. "After that, your indecision becomes a line item."

"We could mix finishes," Tanya offered. "Chrome in baths for easy maintenance, gold brass on living room sconces, oil-rubbed bronze on kitchen pulls."

"Say 'visual interest' and I'll buy you another milkshake," Sue said.

"Visual interest," Tanya replied without shame.

"Two milkshakes," Ellen said, surrendering to the glee of it. "One for bravery."

As if on cue, Bradley slid up beside their booth holding a wireless microphone. He rapped lightly on the table with his knuckles and grinned and, without preamble, launched into a bright, buttery tenor: "In the jungle, the mighty jungle, the lion sleeps tonight . . ."

A handful of diners chuckled and immediately joined on the soft ooooo-weee-oooo backing line. Bradley leaned into the chorus with showman charm, then cupped the mic and tilted it toward their table. "A-wimoweh, a-wimoweh," he coaxed, blue eyes twinkling.

Sue belted first, unembarrassed and glorious, her voice unsurprisingly strong. Ellen felt laughter bubble up and, against her better instincts, she joined, weaving a harmony just under Sue's melody. Tanya threw up her hands as if surrendering to joy and chimed in, off-key and perfect.

Heads turned. The booth behind them clapped to the beat. The toddler with the milkshake shouted "a-wimoweh!" at a decibel level that could shatter glass, and no one minded at all. By the final high "Weeeee-eeeee-eeeeee-eee-eeeee-ohm," the whole diner was a choir.

Bradley bowed, and the room applauded, some with fries still in their hands.

When the applause subsided and Bradley drifted to wait on another table, Ellen leaned back against the red vinyl and watched her friends. Sue was scribbling decisions in her notebook between bites of steak. Tanya was dipping a fry in her milkshake and seemed to be pondering fixture finishes.

Ellen felt the kind of contentment that sneaks up on you after a hard stretch—the good food, the colors decided, the promise of progress humming in her chest. She thought of the house, quiet under the noon light, and of Caleb's sure hands, and of the wild, steep woods beyond where stone teeth waited in the hill.

They would make this place shine, she thought. They would bring light and order and color to rooms that had seen grief. They would do the work—sweat and choices and laughter and one or two singalongs—and the house would reward them with its particular music: warm boards under stockinged feet, a kettle's whistle, the hush of snow against a window.

And if shadows pressed at the edge of all that?

Well. They were not newcomers to shadows.

"Okay," Sue said, stabbing her pen at the granite book like it could hear her. "Decision: Azul Platina. Gray cabinets. We'll live dangerously and decide hardware tomorrow."

"Progress," Ellen said, raising her coffee mug.

Tanya clinked her water glass to Ellen's mug like it was champagne. "To not fainting."

"To singing in public," Sue said.

They laughed, and Bradley, across the room, shot them a two-finger salute mid-bridge of "Fly Me to the Moon," as if to say, "Dream big, ladies."

They intended to.

CHAPTER SIX

Evening at the Condo

After an afternoon of smudging the mansion, ordering cabinets locally, appliance shopping, fixture browsing, and strolling through a local nursery, the three friends treated themselves to a scrumptious dinner at the Devil's Waterfall, a bistro Kimberly Watkins had recommended. By the time they returned to their rental condo, the sky had shifted into deep winter blues, the horizon fringed with the faintest glow from the town's Christmas lights. Now, wrapped in soft robes, they sat in the living room with mugs of hot tea.

Sue, perched in the middle of the couch, leaned over her screen. "Caleb came through. Two estimates." Her tone was matter of fact, but her eyes lit up as she skimmed the details. "I think it's worth it to have him and his crew strip the wallpaper and paint the interior. It'll save us days, maybe weeks, and give us more time to focus on the treasure hunt."

Tanya, curled at one end of the couch, arched a brow. "You say that like finding Alf Bolin's treasure is more important than overseeing the renovations."

"It is," Sue said with mock indignation. "It's the main reason I bought the house."

Ellen smiled into her tea. "Some people collect vintage teacups. We collect hidden treasure."

Sue opened a browser window. "Speaking of which—let's see what more we can find out online." She typed *Alf Bolin treasure* into Google, and up popped a row of YouTube thumbnails, all featuring a familiar face.

"Jason Albright," Sue said. "Should we watch his other videos?"

A chill crept down Ellen's spine as the memory of his dead body in the Victorian mansion blazed behind her eyes.

"Maybe we should listen to what he had to say," Tanya muttered, shifting closer to see the screen.

"We might find a clue about his murderer." Ellen moved closer to Sue, too, sandwiching her between herself and Tanya.

Sue clicked the first video, titled "The Bloody Reign of Alf Bolin."

Jason appeared on-screen, standing before a rocky bluff as dawn light spilled over the treetops.

"Hey, treasure hunters, Jason Albright here. Today we're diving into one of the bloodiest legends in Ozark history, the outlaw Alf Bolin. And let me tell you . . . this guy wasn't some misunderstood Robin Hood. He was a cold-blooded killer."

"Charming," Ellen murmured.

Jason gestured to an old map appearing beside him.

"Bolin was born in Taney County in 1842. When the Civil War broke out, law enforcement all but vanished. Bolin set up here at Murder Rocks, lying in wait above the Springfield–Harrison Road.

"Thirteen confirmed murders—soldiers, settlers, traders. No survivors. And every attack ended the same: the gang stripped their victims of anything valuable and hid it somewhere in these hills."

"I wonder if the ghosts of his victims are still there," Tanya whispered.

Sue's eyes gleamed. "I hope so. Maybe they know where the gold is."

"Sue!" Ellen chastised.

"Only kidding. Of course, I'd rather they be at peace. But if they aren't, maybe they can help, that's all."

The video ended, and the autoplay queued up the next: "The Death of Alf Bolin."

Jason stood at the mouth of a cave, mist curling around jagged rocks.

"Hello, treasure hunters. In today's video, I continue to share my research on Alf Bolin. If you missed Part One, find it linked in the description below.

"Now, back to the man and the legend: Union soldiers chased Bolin for months, but he was a hard rider and a better woodsman. Every time they closed in, he slipped away. So, they came up with a plan to trap him instead.

"Held prisoner was a Confederate soldier named Foster, whose wife lived near the Arkansas–Missouri line, just a few miles south of Murder Rocks. The Union offered her a deal: help capture Bolin, and her husband would go free. Risky for Mrs. Foster? Absolutely. But she agreed.

"They sent a soldier named Zack Thomas to pose as a sick and weary Confederate, staying in the Foster attic for several days. Bolin, as was his habit when in the area, often took his meals at the Foster home. And sure enough, one day he showed up—alone.

"While they were eating, Thomas made a noise upstairs. When Bolin demanded to know who was in the attic, Mrs. Foster told him it was just a poor Southern soldier on his way home. Suspicious, Bolin ordered him to come down, threatening to kill him if he didn't.

"Thomas appeared, weak and slow-moving, and joined them at the table. Bolin kept his pistol close, resting it on the table as he ate. But as the minutes passed, his suspicion cooled. Then he turned his back.

"That's when Thomas grabbed the fire poker and struck him. Bolin went down, but not immediately. Thomas kept hitting until the outlaw was dead. February 1, 1863. Bolin was just twenty-one years old.

"His body was taken to Forsyth. His head was cut off and mounted on a pole in Ozark. And the entire region celebrated."

"Wow," Ellen murmured as the video faded to black. "That's not just killing someone, that's making a point."

"Yep," Sue said. "And it makes me think the ghosts around Murder Rocks have plenty to say."

"He was only twenty-one," Tanya pointed out. "I wonder what made him so cruel at such a young age."

The next video rolled: "The Legend of the Loot."

Jason walked along a wooded trail.

"Missouri during the Civil War was chaos. Neighbors turned against each other. Guerrilla fighters—bushwhackers—prowled the hills, claiming allegiance to one side or the other, but most were just in it for themselves.

"The Ozarks were perfect for them: dense woods, hidden caves, twisting ridges. And in that chaos, Alf Bolin thrived.

"After Bolin's death, rumors spread that he'd buried gold, silver, and loot somewhere in the hills. Some claim it's here, in Murder Rocks, a cave system deep in the Ozarks. Treasure hunters have been searching for over a century, but the terrain is rough and dangerous. People have been injured trying to find it. Still, the lure remains. Maybe it's the idea that the outlaw's ill-gotten gains are just sitting out there, waiting.

"Me? I think there's some truth to it. And I've got my own theories about where to look. Watch next week's video, when I go beneath Murder Rocks to share my theory."

The next video in the queue was the live broadcast they'd already watched—the one featuring his death.

"We need to reach out to Bolin's victims," Sue said. "I bet not all of them moved on."

Ellen raised an eyebrow. "We can help them with that."

Sue grinned. "Exactly. And if they don't know where the treasure is, well, maybe they'll at least point us in the right direction."

Tanya groaned. "So, we're going to ask a bunch of murdered ghosts to help us find treasure stolen by the guy who killed them? Yeah, I'm sure they'll be thrilled."

Ellen laughed but felt a flicker of unease. Treasure hunting was one thing, summoning the dead for directions was another. Still, the mystery tugged at her, the way all their cases did.

"I'd still like to know who killed Jason Albright," Ellen said. "If we can question the ghosts about his murder, count me in. Maybe we can even talk to Jason himself."

"It's a deal," Sue said. Then, turning to Tanya, Sue asked, "You in?"

Tanya laughed. "Of course, as long as I'm not the one doing the heavy lifting."

Sue wrinkled her nose. "I can't make any promises—at least, not until I'm in as good as shape as you."

Ellen sipped her tea and stared at the paused image of Murder Rocks on Sue's laptop, wondering if somewhere out there—under stone, under roots, under decades of secrets—Alf Bolin's treasure was waiting for them.

More importantly, she hoped for answers.

Who killed Jason Albright . . . and why?

Ellen lay in the dark, her noisemaker humming in the silence between Sue's obnoxious snores. She'd just hung up with Brian, his voice still lingering in her ears—warm, steady, comforting. Moseby's little bark had made her smile, and for a moment she'd been able to set everything aside and imagine she was back home, curled up on her own couch with a cup of tea and a quilt over her knees.

But that moment had passed.

She shifted beneath the covers, trying to get comfortable. Despite her efforts to clear her mind, images of Jason Albright's grinning YouTube persona flickered in her head, spliced in with the reality of his lifeless body on that dusty bedroom floor. The videos they'd watched earlier kept replaying—his voice narrating Civil War battles and outlaw escapades, his hand sweeping across the jagged mouth of the Murder Rocks cave like a magician about to reveal his next trick.

Alf Bolin's treasure had been an enticing hook before today, but now Ellen found herself chasing a different thread altogether. The gold and silver—if it even existed—had been hidden for more than a century.

It could wait. But the question of who killed Jason Albright, and why, gnawed at her like a relentless rodent.

Her gaze drifted toward the dim outline of the window across the room. Outside, the moon lit the slope of the distant hills, casting the trees into black silhouettes. Somewhere beyond those ridges and Branson below, the woods stretched all the way to Murder Rocks and the tangle of caves and gullies beneath it. She imagined the darkness there—thicker, heavier, alive with the weight of history and secrets.

Was Jason's killer out there now?

The thought sent a ripple of unease down her spine. She'd seen enough of human nature—and more than enough of the supernatural—to know that evil didn't always stay buried. Sometimes it stuck around, wearing new faces, waiting for its moment.

Ellen rolled onto her side, facing Sue's bed. The dim light from the digital clock painted a soft glow on Sue's peaceful face, her hair fanned out on the pillow. Sue had the kind of courage that burned bright when it was needed, but Ellen knew she could also be reckless. And Sue had made it clear—she wanted that treasure. And if she thought poking around Murder Rocks would get her closer, she'd go, danger or not.

That meant Ellen would be going, too. Of course she would. But she also knew she'd keep her eyes open for anything—anything—that might point them toward Jason's killer.

She thought back to the moment they'd walked into that bedroom three days ago. The sharp, metallic tang in the air. Jason's eyes had been wide open, and that windowpane, long and jagged, had been thrust deep into his chest. She wondered if the police had combed through his videos the way she and her friends had. Maybe there was something there—some clue in the background, some offhand comment that meant nothing to most viewers but might mean everything to the right set of eyes.

A soft creak echoed in the condo—just the building settling, she told herself. But she found her hand resting on her phone anyway, as if she could call Brian back and somehow have him talk her through the night. Instead, she closed her eyes and tried to focus on his earlier words: *Don't worry too much, El. Enjoy your trip. Let the police handle it.*

Easier said than done.

The truth was, she *did* want to enjoy the trip. She wanted to see Sue happy in her new home, to help bring the Victorian back to life. She wanted to take the hikes and visit the quirky diners and stand on the lip of that cave and feel like she'd touched a piece of history.

But she also wanted answers. She wanted to know why a young man with a knack for storytelling had ended up dead in an empty house. She wanted to know if he'd stumbled into something more dangerous than he could handle—or if someone had led him straight to it.

And she wanted to know if that someone was still close by.

Another creak. This one sharper. Ellen's eyes opened to the dark again, her heartbeat picking up. She listened for Sue's snores . . . still steady. No footsteps, no voices. Just the faint hum of the heater. She let out the breath she'd been holding, feeling a little foolish.

Still, she thought as she rolled back over, she hoped to talk to ghosts, to get answers.

Somewhere out there, pieces of the puzzle were waiting. Whether they led to gold, justice, or danger, she wasn't sure. But come morning, she and her friends would be one step closer to finding out.

Ellen pulled the covers up to her chin and closed her eyes. She told herself she was ready for whatever lay ahead.

She hoped she was right.

CHAPTER SEVEN

A Hunt and a Hoedown

Ellen, Sue, and Tanya pulled into the gravel driveway beside the Victorian mansion. Caleb's truck was already parked near the porch, its bed piled high with ladders, tarps, and paint cans. A huge trailer was parked in front of it and was already filled with demolished cabinets and at least one sink.

They stepped outside into the early December chill. The afternoon sun shone from high noon as Ellen, full from their early lunch, followed Sue and Tanya up the porch steps and into the house where the air smelled faintly of plaster dust and old wood.

Caleb appeared from the hallway, wearing his work jeans, a hoodie dusted with white, and a ball cap. "Morning, ladies," he said, wiping his hands on a rag. "We're moving right along. Wallpaper's half down upstairs. The plaster's in decent shape under most of it—better than I expected for a place this old."

Sue beamed. "That's good news. So, you're okay to start painting soon?"

"Should be. We'll get the last of the demolition done today, give it a coat of primer. We'll be set." He glanced toward the back door. "When should we expect tile, cabinets, and countertops to arrive?"

"I put in my order yesterday. The cabinets aren't custom, so they'll be here tomorrow, and the tile and countertops should arrive by Friday—Monday at the latest. I've made most of my other selections already, too."

He gave a curt nod. "Treasure hunting today?" His lips twitched into an amused smile as he glanced over their backpacks and flashlights.

"Paranormal investigating," Tanya corrected, as if the title lent gravity to what they were about to do.

"Right," Caleb said, eyes twinkling. "Just be careful. Those rocks have a way of breaking ankles."

Ellen slung her backpack over one shoulder. "We'll be fine. We have a plan."

They did. Sort of.

They followed the same faint deer path that Kimberly had led them down two days ago, crunching through frosty leaves. The tall trees made the sky look bigger and further away, making Ellen feel small.

Sue led the way. Ellen was impressed by Sue's stamina and endurance, built up by three months of walking the casino floor on the Blackfeet reservation. She'd lost seventy-five pounds—and more since then—and could move as fast as Ellen now. They moved quietly, each step taking them deeper into the hush of the woods, until Ellen broke the silence.

"I've been meaning to ask you, Sue . . . are you over your gambling addiction for good? Or do you still watch *Mo Mummy* on YouTube?"

Sue stopped and turned to face Tanya and Ellen, who also stopped in their tracks. "Do you want the truth?" she asked.

Ellen's stomach turned.

"Always," Tanya said.

Sue continued down the trail, perhaps wanting to tell her truth without looking at them. "I've flown out to the casino a few times. More than a few."

"Oh, no," Ellen said so softly that the others may not have heard.

"A few weeks ago, Tom closed our accounts and transferred our money into an account in his name only. I agreed to it."

"Oh, gosh, Sue," Tanya said. "Are you getting help? Like with a therapist?"

"I promised to start after this trip," she said as they neared Murder Rocks.

Murder Rocks was a jumbled collection of limestone outcroppings, their edges jagged, faces mottled with lichen. Some stood stacked like crude fortresses; others formed natural walls, pocked with crevices and shadowed hollows.

Beneath them was supposed to be a cave system where Alf Bolin and his crew hid out.

As the three friends took off their backpacks and got out their equipment, Sue continued, "I have a credit card for all my expenses, which Tom thinks is safe because you can't use credit cards at the casino, and this card doesn't have the cash advance feature."

"But it isn't safe?" Ellen asked.

Sue shook her head. "Just last weekend, I went shopping with Lexi and asked her to let me use my credit card for her purchases so she could give me the cash. I want one last hurrah before I quit."

"But how much have you lost?" Tanya asked. "More than the initial thirty grand?"

"Another fifteen," Sue admitted. "Which is why I'm so desperate to find this treasure. I need to make it up to Tom."

"Fifteen *grand*?" Ellen repeated. "To total forty-five lost?"

"It's not about the money," Tanya argued. "We have plenty from the oil and the gold we found at the Gold House. It's about you needing help."

"It's about the money, too," Sue insisted. "Have you noticed that the oil money is thinning out? It's not going to last much longer. And the way we spend it on these trips on top of what I've lost . . ." Sue's voice trailed off.

"The only way to make it up to Tom is to fight the addiction," Ellen said. "You're finding ways to *feed* it."

Ellen set the spirit box on a flattish rock and switched it on. The static-filled scanning began, the machine cycling rapidly through radio frequencies.

Sue turned to them with a tear-stained face. "I used my charity money. That's how I defended myself to Tom. It was money going to charity, so no loss to him. But I feel so selfish." Sue covered her face and sobbed.

Ellen and Tanya put down their equipment and put their arms around Sue.

"It's a sickness," Tanya said in a comforting tone. "You just need help, that's all."

"You're a good person, Sue," Ellen reminded her.

"That's not what Tom's brother, Kyle, says." Sue wiped her tears from her cheeks.

"What do you mean?" Tanya gazed down at Sue with fierce eyes.

"Apparently, Kyle thought he should talk to Luke about my gambling addiction, and when Luke tried to defend me, Kyle said that he could tell Luke twenty-seven bad things about me, if Luke was prepared to hear them."

"What?" Ellen stepped back and covered her heart. "Why would Kyle say something like that to *your son?*"

"And where in the world did he come up with that number?" Tanya said with a shake of her blonde ponytail.

Sue shrugged. "He's always been the black sheep of Tom's family, so I guess it was a chance for him to feel on top by bad-mouthing me."

"I'm sure Luke considered the source," Tanya put in.

"That might not go in my favor," Sue said with an exaggerated frown.

"Well, I don't know," Ellen began with a grin. "Tanya and I know you better than anyone, and I can only think of *seventeen* bad things about you."

Sue lifted her chin and laughed out loud.

"If we find the treasure," Tanya added after a beat, "just give at least ten percent to charity. I've already decided on St. Jude's."

"*If* we find it?" Sue asked with reproach. "*When* we find it. It's the only way I can redeem myself to Tom."

Ellen knew that wasn't true, but instead of arguing, she said, "Then we better get started."

Tanya put on her headphones and plugged them into the EVP recorder before putting her microphone in the air. "I'm ready."

Sue took up her full-spectrum camera and pointed it toward the mouth of the caves. "Ready."

After putting a Mini Maglite at that interim place between on and off and laying it on the rock across from her, Ellen lifted her SLS camera and said, "Spirits of the other realm, this is Ellen, Sue, and Tanya. We come in peace and mean no harm. We'd like to speak with anyone here who knew Alf Bolin—either as a member of his gang or as one of his victims."

Static crackled, and then—clear enough to raise goosebumps—a man's voice broke through: "Hello."

Sue and Tanya exchanged wide-eyed looks.

"Who are we speaking with?" Ellen asked just as she picked up a figure on her SLS camera. It was crouched on the highest rock.

A pause. Then: "James."

"James, do you know who killed Jason Albright?"

"Who?"

"Jason Albright," Sue nearly shouted.

"No."

The three friends frowned at one another.

Then Sue asked, "Did you know Alf Bolin?"

The spirit box crackled, followed by a string of unintelligible sounds.

"Can you say that again?" Ellen asked.

They waited but heard nothing but static from the box.

"Is there anyone else here from the spirit world?" Sue asked.

"Maybe Jason Albright?" Ellen added. "By any chance, are you here with us? We're eager to know what happened to you."

Another voice cut in, this one deeper, raspier: "Okay."

"Is this Jason?" Ellen asked with wide eyes.

The spirit box hissed, "No, no, no."

"Who are you?" Sue asked. "Can you tell us your name?"

The name that came through wasn't clear, but it sounded like "Elijah."

Ellen lifted her brows. "Elijah? Is that your name?"

"Yeah."

Ellen showed the others a second stick figure that had emerged on her SLS screen.

Sue turned in the direction of the figures. "Elijah, did you know Alf Bolin?"

The spirit box crackled. "Yes."

The three friends exchanged looks of excitement.

"Do you know where he buried his treasure?" Sue asked.

"No."

Sue sighed. "This isn't going very well, is it," she said without inflection.

The spirit box hissed and groaned. "Only one."

"Only one what?" Ellen wondered out loud.

"Knows," the spirit box hissed.

Sue's back straightened. "Knows where the treasure is?"

"Sawyer," the spirit box said.

Tanya tilted her head. "Who's Sawyer?"

Ellen felt the cool air get colder as a breeze blew past.

The spirit box hissed but made no intelligible sound.

"Do you need help moving on?" Tanya asked.

They listened, but there was nothing but static from the box.

The forest seemed to lean closer. Ellen took a breath. "Can we speak with Sawyer? Is he here? Sawyer?"

The static deepened, and then—so faint Ellen thought she imagined it—another voice: "Go away."

"Is this Sawyer?" Sue asked. "Or Alf Bolin?"

A loud crack echoed from above. Ellen's gaze snapped upward just as a boulder, dislodged from the top of the rock formation, hurtled down toward them.

"Move!" Tanya shouted.

They dove sideways, the boulder slamming into the ground where Ellen had been standing seconds before.

"Let's get out of here," Tanya cried, her voice high and tight.

They collected their bags and scrambled back toward the trail, equipment clattering, breath puffing white in the air. Ellen's heart thumped hard, but she couldn't help herself from glancing back as she shoved her equipment into her bag, half expecting to see a shadowy figure in the rocks.

They didn't stop until the mansion came into view.

"Could a ghost have done that?" Tanya said as she took a seat on the porch steps to catch her breath.

Sue bent over her knees, panting. "Like you said before, maybe a vengeful spirit."

Ellen slung her bag over her shoulder. "If he thinks we're giving up, he's got another thing coming."

The Shepherd of the Hills dinner theater was warm, cozy, and already buzzing with the murmur of guests as the three friends were shown to their table. Red-and-green lights twinkled above the stage, and the set— a rustic saloon with swinging doors and a Christmas tree—glowed under soft spotlights.

The smell of pumpkin pie drifted through the room, and Ellen's stomach rumbled.

"Not as crowded as I thought it would be," Ellen said to her friends, who sat on either side of her, facing the stage.

"It's only Wednesday," Sue pointed out. "I bet they draw larger crowds on the weekend."

Dinner was hearty: turkey, dressing, mashed potatoes, gravy, green beans, and rolls, followed by generous wedges of pie. Ellen sipped her tea as the lights dimmed and the actors bustled onto the stage, decked out in cowboy boots, Santa hats, and period garb.

The plot unfolded fast—a Wild West Christmas party gone wrong, complete with shady characters, hidden motives, and an eventual "murder."

It felt good to laugh after what they had endured at Murder Rocks.

Halfway through, the host strolled into the audience, scanning the tables. "We need a volunteer," he announced. "Someone with a knack for sleuthing . . . or at least a good poker face."

Sue pointed at herself with mock innocence. "Who, me?"

"You, ma'am," the host said, beckoning.

Sue was whisked onto the stage, crowned with a massive, feathered hat, and handed a "secret" clue on a scrap of paper. She clutched it to her chest as if it were the Magna Carta.

"My word," she gasped in an exaggerated Southern drawl, "this information is so scandalous, I can hardly bear it!" She fluttered her fake lashes at the fake sheriff and then grasped his arm as though she might swoon. "I must tell you privately before I perish from the shame!"

The audience howled. Tanya, usually the quietest of the three, snorted so loudly her tea went down the wrong pipe. Ellen pressed a napkin to her mouth, trying—and failing—to contain her laughter.

When Sue tiptoed across the stage, bent double as if sneaking, the entire theater dissolved into chaos.

"That woman is fearless," Ellen whispered, tears in her eyes.

"She's going to demand a standing ovation at breakfast tomorrow," Tanya wheezed.

"Tomorrow?" Ellen repeated. "I bet she demands it tonight, right here."

"Let's just promise each other that we'll never let her live this down," Tanya said with a glint in her eyes.

"Deal."

Sue returned to the table triumphant, fanning herself with the clue. "You may now refer to me as *the star of the show*."

"You're insufferable," Ellen said, laughing.

"Insufferably talented," Sue corrected. She doffed the feathered hat at them before plopping it on Tanya's head.

The rest of the show passed in a blur of laughter, gunshot sound effects, and Christmas carols sung off-key by outlaws. When the "murderer" was revealed, the audience gasped, then erupted into applause.

As the lights came up, the three women leaned together, still grinning.

"Okay," Tanya said, dabbing her eyes. "That was worth the price of admission."

"Best comedy I've seen in years," Ellen agreed.

Sue flipped her hair. "It wouldn't have been nearly as good without me in it."

When the curtain closed and the crowd began shuffling toward the exits, Sue slid the feathered hat she'd been given back onto her head and strutted toward the door like a showgirl. She gave a dramatic bow to the cold night air as they stepped outside.

"Thank you, thank you, I'll be here all week," she said, loud enough to turn a few heads in the parking lot.

Ellen rolled her eyes, tugging her coat tighter against the chill. "Please don't encourage her."

But Tanya snorted, covering her mouth to stifle laughter. "Oh, let her have her moment. It's cheaper than therapy."

Their laughter carried them the rest of the way to the Chevy Onix. Ellen's cheeks still ached from smiling as she slid into the driver's seat, but Tanya's expression had grown thoughtful again, her brows knitting in the glow of the dashboard lights.

"I've been thinking," Tanya began as she slid in beside her.

"Ruh-roh," Sue said from the back seat, mimicking Astro from *The Jetsons*.

Ellen chuckled, but Tanya ignored the joke. "That boulder didn't topple on its own today. Wouldn't you agree?"

The smile drained from Ellen's face. She turned the key in the ignition but didn't put the car in gear. "Do you think someone was out there with us?" she asked. "Or do you think it was a ghost protecting the treasure?"

"At first, I assumed ghost," Tanya admitted. "But now, I'm not so sure. A person could've been watching us. Waiting."

"Either way," Sue muttered, buckling her seatbelt, "it felt way too deliberate."

Ellen pulled out her phone. "Maybe we should ask Colton to send someone out there again. I've got his number."

"Good idea," Tanya agreed, her voice clipped.

The phone rang twice before the deputy's voice answered, gruff and unmistakable. "Colton."

"Hello, Deputy, this is Ellen McManius."

"Hi there, Ellen. Funny you should call—I was just about to reach out to you with some news."

"Oh? Let me put you on speaker so Sue and Tanya can hear." Ellen pressed the button and set the phone in the console. "Okay, go ahead, Deputy. We're listening."

"Hello, ladies," Colton said, his tone calm and measured. "Just wanted to let you know the coroner has ruled Albright's death a suicide."

The car went silent. Ellen glanced at Tanya, whose jaw tightened, and then at Sue, who mouthed *what?* from the back seat.

"How can that be?" Ellen asked finally. "You saw the video."

"I did," Colton said. "But the coroner found no other fingerprints or DNA on the shard of glass other than Albright's. Even with gloves, fibers would've shown up. The bloody prints were his, and they were positioned in a way that's consistent with self-infliction."

"That's . . . hard to believe," Sue said.

"I thought you ladies would be relieved," Colton countered, his voice dipping with a trace of skepticism.

"But the video—" Tanya started.

"Must have been an act," the deputy interrupted. "Maybe he wanted to go out with a bang. Stranger things have happened."

"Thanks for the update," Ellen said, though her stomach knotted. "Does this mean the case is closed?"

"Indeed, it does," Colton replied. "No evidence to contradict the coroner's findings."

"Right. Thanks again. Goodbye, then." Ellen ended the call and sat back.

"What do y'all think about that?" she asked after a beat.

"I think it answers one question," Tanya said slowly. "Whoever did that to Jason wasn't alive." Her voice dropped as she turned to Sue. "Do you think your house is safe? Was the cleansing enough?"

"Not as long as we're hunting for the treasure," Ellen put in, the words sharper than she meant. "We don't want to end up like Jason."

"We can't let that ghost win," Sue said firmly. "We'll find out who he is, track down his bones, and burn them. Force him to the other side."

Tanya gave a shaky laugh. "Well, when you say it like that, it almost sounds easy."

Ellen tightened her grip on the wheel, staring through the windshield into the dark. "What choice do we have? Treasure or no treasure, I won't feel safe in that house until he's gone."

Sue leaned back, her hat tilted at a rakish angle. "So, we know what we have to do next, right?"

"Right," Ellen agreed.

"But not tomorrow," Tanya objected. "You promised we'd go to Silver Dollar City for the day."

"Of course," Sue removed her hat. "But after that, we get busy."

CHAPTER EIGHT

Silver Dollar City

The morning light poured through the blinds of the condo, striping the kitchen table where Sue had spread out Caleb's sketches. A mug of coffee steamed beside her elbow, and she peered at the lines and numbers as though deciphering a treasure map.

"These cabinets are going to make the kitchen sing," Sue said, tapping a penciled square with her finger. "Gray shaker with gold hardware. Yes, I decided on gold. Happy, Tanya?"

"You sound like an HGTV host," Ellen teased, sliding a plate of scrambled eggs and toast in front of her friend.

Tanya, who had just padded in wearing fuzzy socks and her hair in a loose braid, smirked. "Yes, I am. It feels good to be heard."

Sue sniffed. "Smells delicious. Thanks, Ellen. I've worked up an appetite calling in all these orders. Oh, and Caleb said my measurements were flawless."

"Of course they were," Ellen said, hiding a grin. "You measured eight times and cut never."

Sue stuck out her tongue, but the sparkle in her eyes betrayed her pride.

Once they had finished their breakfast, the three friends gathered coats and scarves. Ellen stuffed a thermos of hot coffee into her bag, certain they'd need it later, and they piled into their rented Chevy Onix.

"Silver Dollar City, here we come," Sue said from the back seat. "I hope y'all are ready for Christmas on steroids."

"I thought we already had Christmas on steroids last night at the dinner theater," Ellen muttered. "If Santa shows up riding a buffalo, I'm leaving."

"Since when did you turn into Ebeneezer Scrooge?" Tanya teased from the front passenger's seat.

Ellen laughed but didn't admit that she was feeling anxious about the ghost haunting Sue's new property. Was it really capable of murdering the living?

The moment they stepped through the gates, Ellen felt as though she'd entered a Christmas card. Strings of lights glittered across rooftops, every lamppost shimmered with garlands, and every storefront window sparkled with ornaments, nutcrackers, and candy canes. The smell of kettle corn mingled with the sweetness of cinnamon bread and the smokiness of turkey legs turning on spits.

Ellen inhaled deeply, letting her guard down. "If heaven has a food court, this is it."

Sue clasped her gloved hands together. "I told you it would be magical."

"It's magical, all right," Tanya said, eyeing a group of carolers singing beside a giant Christmas tree. "Magically overpriced. Don't say I didn't warn you when that kettle corn costs more than my last electric bill."

"Now who's the Scrooge?" Ellen teased.

They wandered cobblestone streets lined with rustic shops and craftspeople blowing glass ornaments, hammering iron, and dipping candles. Children in knitted hats darted past with mugs of cocoa, their laughter rising like music above the murmur of the crowd.

Ellen felt a warmth bloom in her chest. After Murder Rocks and Jason Albright's chilling videos, it was a relief to walk amid joy.

By noon, they joined the line for the Frisco Silver Dollar Line Steam Train. Its black engine gleamed beneath the winter sun, and its whistle let out a sound that vibrated through Ellen's chest, both nostalgic and thrilling. They boarded, sliding into a bench of polished wood.

"I love trains," Ellen said, glancing out at the pine-covered hills.

"I do, too," Tanya admitted. "We should ride the one in Branson. There's something romantic about them, don't you think?"

"Romantic?" Sue arched a brow. "This bench feels like sitting on a two-by-four."

The train jolted into motion, chugging along tracks that curved through the Ozarks. Steam puffed into the sky, and families waved as the cars clattered past. Ellen relaxed into the rhythm of the ride, the sound of wheels against rails soothing in its steadiness.

Until the bushwhackers arrived.

Two men in ragged cowboy hats leapt onto the train, waving sticks in the air. "This here's a stickup!" one hollered, his voice booming. "Get it?" He pointed to his stick. "Stick *up?*"

Children squealed with delight. Parents clapped.

"Hand over yer gold!"

When the second outlaw introduced himself as *Alf Bolin*, Ellen's stomach dropped.

The name rang through the air like a gunshot.

"Did he just say—" Tanya began.

"Yep," Sue whispered. "That's our guy."

The outlaw prowled down the aisle, mock-scowling at passengers. "Don't try any tricks, folks. I'm the meanest bushwhacker this side of the Mississippi!"

Tanya rolled her eyes. "I can't believe we're being robbed by a community theater version of our ghost."

The bushwhackers stomped back toward the caboose, their act ending with exaggerated bows. The train resumed its steady journey, but Ellen couldn't shake the unease curling through her. First the murder mystery dinner, now this—two nights in a row, entertainment too close to their own troubles. Coincidence, or a sign?

The rest of the afternoon was a whirlwind.

They explored *Marvel Cave*, descending into cool, echoing chambers glittering with limestone formations. Ellen marveled at the cathedral-sized space while Sue muttered about bats. Tanya, surprisingly, seemed more fascinated than frightened.

They wandered through the Craftsman's Valley, watching artisans mold silver jewelry and carve wooden toys. Ellen bought a hand-painted ornament shaped like a cardinal, imagining it on her tree back home.

Then Sue dragged them to *Fire in the Hole*, an indoor rollercoaster. "Come on! It's historical!" she insisted.

"Historical doesn't mean safe," Tanya protested, clutching the safety bar as the car lurched forward. Her shriek echoed through the dark as the ride plummeted down its first drop.

When they stumbled out, Tanya clutched her stomach. "I swear I saw my soul leave my body."

"If it did," Ellen said, smirking, "it probably went shopping without you."

Sue grinned. "At least you didn't puke on the historical scenery."

As twilight settled over the park and thousands of Christmas lights flickered on, the three women ducked into a sprawling gift shop. Shelves overflowed with ornaments, cookbooks, and Ozark souvenirs. Ellen trailed her fingers over a quilted throw, admiring its intricate stitching.

"This quilt would look lovely over a chair in your new reading nook," Ellen called to Sue.

"Hey," Sue called back, holding up a thick paperback. "Look at this."

The title blared in bold letters: *Murder Rocks: Alf Bolin and the Civil War*, by Woody P. Snow.

Ellen's breath caught.

The cover featured sepia-toned figures in Confederate garb, rifles slung across their shoulders, with a rugged man at the forefront. His eyes burned with intensity, his jaw set in defiance.

Tanya frowned. "What are the odds?"

"Apparently pretty high," Sue said, flipping the book over. "It's got pictures, too."

Ellen reached for it, her fingers tingling as she touched the cover. "We have to buy this."

Tanya muttered, "Define *have to*."

"Knowledge is power," Ellen reminded her. "And if Alf's ghost is really haunting your house, Sue, we need to understand him better."

Sue plopped the book on the counter with a grin. "Light bedtime reading, coming right up."

By the time they reached Buckshot Annie's Skillet Cookery, the air smelled of sizzling sausage and peppers. The three women squeezed into a wooden booth and ordered hearty skillets piled high with potatoes, onions, and cornbread.

When the food arrived, steaming and savory, Ellen cracked open the book. She skimmed a few pages and read aloud:

"'Though Alf Bolin has often been painted as a ruthless killer, some accounts suggest he was a victim of circumstance—pressed into violence by the chaos of the Civil War, his youth twisted by bloodshed and poverty. He was only twenty-one when he met his end.'"

Tanya set down her fork with a scowl. "Oh, please. Everyone had it rough during the war. That doesn't excuse murdering innocent settlers."

"Maybe Woody P. Snow is trying to get him a Netflix redemption arc," Sue said, spearing a sausage. "Alf: The Musical."

Ellen frowned, rereading the passage. "It does make me wonder, though. If his ghost is still here, maybe it's not just about treasure. Maybe he's tethered by unfinished business, or by the way people remember him."

Tanya sipped her tea. "Well, I'm not about to throw him a pity party. He's dangerous, even in death."

Ellen turned to Tanya. "Aren't you the one who always says we shouldn't judge a person by what they do after death?"

Tanya shifted in her seat. "No, I think that was you. Besides, he did murder people before his death, too."

"We don't even know if our ghost is Alf Bolin," Sue pointed out.

They agreed to read more of the book together that evening back at the condo. Ellen couldn't shake the sense that it would be important—that understanding Alf Bolin's humanity might reveal why his spirit still lingered, if, in fact, it did.

As they stepped back into the night, Silver Dollar City glowed under a blanket of lights. Carols drifted from hidden speakers, families strolled with cocoa, and the scent of peppermint filled the air.

Yet Ellen felt a chill.

"First a murder mystery dinner, now Alf Bolin robbing our train," she murmured as they headed toward the car.

Sue looped her arm through hers. "The Ozarks are trying to tell us something."

Tanya pulled her scarf tighter. "Let's just hope they wait until after dessert."

Their laughter rang out, but beneath it, Ellen felt the pull of something deeper—like shadows hiding beneath twinkling lights. And in her bag, the book weighed heavier than paper should, promising answers they weren't sure they wanted.

CHAPTER NINE

Alf Bolin

The condo had settled into that delicious evening hush that only comes after a long day—the air warm, the lamps low, and Branson's glittering lights winking beyond the balcony like a scattered constellation. Ellen padded across the living room in fuzzy socks. She'd changed into plaid pajama bottoms and a soft, heather-gray T-shirt that read "Readers Do it in the Margins." Steam curled from the mugs she'd lined up on the coffee table: chamomile for Tanya, peppermint for Sue, and a cinnamon blend for herself.

Sue emerged from the hallway in a satin robe the color of eggplant and an old Sooners tee underneath, carrying the prize they'd brought home from Silver Dollar City—the thick paperback with its sepia cover and the bold title, *Murder Rocks: Alf Bolin and the Civil War.* She dropped onto the end of the couch with theatrical care, as if the book were a relic.

"Moment of truth," Sue said, smoothing the cover. "Are we ready to meet the man behind our very festive nightmares?"

Tanya sank onto the couch beside Sue, knees folded under her, ponytail looped low. "As ready as I'll ever be to spend my Friday night cuddling up with a murderer."

Ellen sat on the opposite end of the couch, positioning Sue in between them, and sipped her cinnamon tea.

Sue flipped open to the table of contents. The paper smelled faintly of glue and ink, that particular perfume of new books. The chapter headings marched down the page—Bolin's Beginnings; Bushwhacker Country; The Springfield-Harrison Road; Murder Rocks; Louisa; The Trap; The Head on the Pike.

"Louisa," Tanya said softly, tapping the page. "That's the one I want. If we understand her, maybe we'll understand him."

Sue made a face. "Is understanding him the goal? Because I'm more of a 'banish him' kind of girl."

Ellen rubbed her chin. "We can do both. Learn first, banish later."

Sue thumbed to the chapter on Louisa. The font was small but crisp, the paragraphs tight. A black-and-white photo was printed above the text: a hillside eaten by scrub and rock. The image itself looked innocuous—light on stone, shadows pooled in creases—but a pulse of dread ran through Ellen anyway, as if the photograph hummed at a pitch only she could hear.

She remembered the bushwhacker on the park train calling himself Alf. Even though it had been a scripted joke, her body had tensed as if a wire had tightened around her ribs. Coins clinking together in a canvas sack. A hat brim low over eyes. Hoofbeats.

"Read," Tanya prompted, in the same tone she used when she was trying not to fidget.

Sue cleared her throat and began, her voice taking on the cadence she used when she told ghost stories to skeptical contractors. "Alf was seventeen when Louisa came to stay with the Bilyeus—the family that had taken in Alf and his sister, Annabel, when they were seven and five," she read. "Louisa's parents, slave owners, had been killed when a gang of abolitionists raided their farm and burned it down. She was twenty years old and had vibrant red curls that were as explosive as her personality."

Ellen pictured the girl not as a faded figure from the past but as a body in motion—a flash of copper hair, a grin that dared you to be bored. But it was hard to feel sorry for a family of slave owners. Sometimes freeing a group of oppressed people meant casualties.

"A cousin from Little Rock sent her newspapers to keep her abreast of current events," Sue continued. "She impressed Alf when she read him an article from the *Arkansas True Democrat* entitled 'War Storms Brewing at Missouri-Kansas Border.' Smoldering with rage, Louisa said to him, 'Missouri is being attacked from all sides except the south, and if you just sit here and do nothing, the so-called Free-Soilers will make their way here and kill us all.' Then, she added, 'I'm a fighter and would gladly risk my life for the South. Will you?' It says here that 'although not much is known about her outside of Alf Bolin's letters, what seems certain is that she and Alf were bound by strong political convictions— something that would send them running across state lines with two brothers in tow, all four of them making themselves useful to the secessionists.'"

"There are letters?" Ellen's brows shot up.

"I think much of this book is based on them." Sue turned to the back of the book. "Here. It just says 'the letters of Alf Bolin.'"

"I wonder if they still exist?" Tanya put in.

Ellen did a quick Google search. "I can't find anything on Google."

"Maybe the local library will know," Tanya suggested.

"Let's get back to the book." Ellen nodded at Sue, beckoning her to continue.

"They thought themselves heroes," Sue said. "Louisa, in particular, believed—so the author says—that courage meant action without fear. They undermined Union supply lines, passed information, did the things young people do when they believe the world is a clear map and they've got the legend." She glanced up. "Legend as in the key, not the other kind."

"I understood," Ellen said, smiling.

Tanya's mouth twisted. "Idealists with guns. That's never gone wrong."

Sue read on: "But war eats ideals for breakfast. One afternoon, Alf came upon Louisa on a hillside—" Sue's voice faltered. She cleared her throat and tried again. "He found her hurt. Bruised. Her scalp singed—the red hair scorched to the skin. The book is blunt about it. She was raped and tortured, and the men who did it called themselves Secesh."

Silence fell like a heavy curtain. The heater kicked on with a whisper, then settled. Beyond the balcony, someone laughed on a neighboring patio, a sound so normal Ellen wanted to throw a pillow at the glass to startle it away.

She felt Tanya shift, the chair's cushion sighing. "Torture is bad enough, but when it's done to you by your own side—" Tanya paused, unable to find words. Then, she finally said, "Secessionists did that to her, men on the side they were fighting for."

"Or the men who wore the right colors but had no sides at all," Ellen said quietly.

Tanya's mouth had hardened into a thin line. "Either way, it must have broken something in him."

Sue read on, more softly now. "After Louisa died—and she did die, not long after, the text says—Alf changed. He gathered men in the hills. He called them Merry Men. His cause became Missouri and Missourians—protecting them from armies on both sides, or so he told himself. He'd free the state of marauders, he said, and plunder both Blue and Gray." Sue looked up at Ellen. "Protecting by plundering. How very reassuring."

Ellen turned the words over. Hero and villain. Victim and avenger. If you looked from one angle, the lines made a tiger. From another, a vase. She thought of Sawyer—the name rolling around her head like a dropped marble, the way the spirit box had hissed *leave*—and it felt suddenly important that Louisa had come before everything. Like a key in a lock.

"Does it say how old she was when she died?" Ellen asked.

"Let's see," Sue scanned. "Twenty when she arrived at the Bilyeus and twenty-two when she died. The young and reckless years."

"Her hair," Tanya said, "the detail about the singeing, it's so—" She rubbed at her temple, searching for the word. "Specific."

It was specific, and in its specificity, it was awful. Ellen pictured a hand holding a flame close enough to burn but not burn out. She felt the old animal part of her brain wake up, ready to bite or bolt. Every ghost they'd ever dealt with had left something behind—a scratched message, a cold draft, a door opening and closing. But the ones who burned hot, the ones who haunted, not because they were lonely but because they were furious, were the dangerous ones. Those bled into the land.

"Oh, look," Sue said suddenly, pointing to a page in the book. "It's a letter written by Alf to his sister, Annabel. Apparently, she lived at a school for the blind in Springfield."

"I suppose someone read her letters to her," Tanya offered.

"I suppose so," Sue said. "Listen: 'Dear Annabel, I received your letter full of your concerns. Remember that story I told you about Robin Hood? Folks called him a bushwhacker, too. He robbed from the rich to make the world a fairer place, and with this Kansas-Nebraska Act, rich northerners are pouring money and abolitionists into Kansas to sneak across the border and rob and rape and kill us Missourians. It was an abolitionist that killed Pa, you know. Maybe you don't recall. You were only three. Mom died two years later, so, in a way, the abolitionist killed her, too. The point is what these people are doing is sickening. I'm doing what I can to help keep Missouri free. I'm doing God's work, just like the night I killed the man who was climbing on top of you. Your brother, Alf.'"

"He really did see himself as a hero," Ellen muttered with incredulity.

"Either that," Sue began, "or that's what he wanted his sister to believe."

"I'm so glad we weren't living back then," Tanya said with a shake of her ponytail. "Can you imagine? Fathers and sons on different sides. Neighbors. No one knew who their allies really were. People getting raped and murdered, their farms burned down. It was chaos."

"Keep going," Ellen said to Sue, softly.

Sue turned the page. The paper rasped like dry leaves across pavement.

"It talks about the road," she said. "The Springfield-Harrison—its curve, the way Murder Rocks presses up under it like a shoulder under cloth. It says the incline and the trees gave men like Alf cover and a vantage point, and that the limestone's face—pocked and layered—hid alcoves where a boy could become a shadow and do a man's violence."

Sue's thumb paused halfway down the page. "There's a paragraph here," she said, "about loyalty. How the author pieced together an image of Alf's right-hand man—a kid, fourteen maybe, who adored him, who would do anything for him. He'd been taken in, the text suggests, like a stray—fed by Alf and given a purpose. The boy stood lookout, tracked horses, ran messages, and when men in the gang asked about their share of the loot, he made examples of them."

"Sawyer," Ellen said, before she realized she'd done it.

Sue grimaced. "The boy with the rifle. The one who killed anyone who asked where the treasure was."

"Only one other person ever knew besides Alf," Tanya whispered, repeating the spirit box's gift from that afternoon. "Only Sawyer."

"So, he was both witness and executioner," Sue said. "I bet he's our ghost, and no wonder he's not big on visitors."

Ellen sat back against the cushions and stared at the ceiling, where light pooled in gentle circles from the floor lamp. If Louisa's death was the key, then Sawyer was the lock that clicked after. Ellen imagined him with winter-chapped lips and a coat too big; imagined hands that shook until they didn't anymore. A teenager. A boy who could convince himself that killing was just a darker name for protecting—until the words were interchangeable.

"Does it say anything else about Louisa?" Ellen asked. "What she said to Alf, at the end?"

Sue flipped a few pages, scanning, then shook her head. "No recorded last words. Just the gist—she told him who hurt her."

"Secesh," Tanya said again, and looked as if she wanted to wash her mouth out after.

If Louisa had died with some fragment of a plea in her mouth, it hadn't traveled across time. What they were left with were the facts that made men into legends: a boy, a girl, a hillside; a group rape, hair singed, a promise made, a road haunted.

Sue placed her finger under the next paragraph and read: "'It's tempting to sand Bolin's edges down—to imagine him as something easily understood: a vigilante pushed too far. But the records also list dead men and stolen payrolls, slaughtered travelers and homes ransacked. The outlaw may have told himself he'd save Missouri from both sides, but the dead weren't saved.'"

"That's the thing about motive," Tanya said, her voice gentler than her words. "It's a great story. Until someone ends up in the ground."

Ellen nodded. The words did a strange double-dutch in her head—two ropes swinging, overlapping, the jump between them dangerous. It was a relief to feel Tanya's clarity in the room like a plumb line.

Sue took a deep breath. "There's more about the ambushes and the treasure." She tilted the page toward the lamp. "Some of the payrolls were silver, some gold. There's a scrap of testimony from a man who swore he saw bars—a stack of them—before he ran for his life. The author says that rumor and fact braided together so tightly you can't always tell which is which. But the treasure's repeated like a chorus."

"And the chorus keeps bringing men back to the same verse," Ellen said. "Murder Rocks."

The name sat heavy. Even here in their soft pajamas, wrapped in lamplight, the phrase altered the shape of the night.

Sue let the book fall closed in her lap and curled her fingers around her mug. "It paints him complicated," she said. "I can feel that—and I don't want to. I want him simple. Evil, so we can salt him like a slug and be done with it."

"I know." Tanya took a gulp of chamomile, then made a face when it burned. "And if that boy—Sawyer—believed he was protecting what Louisa died for—"

"Then he believes it still," Sue said. "And he doesn't care who gets hurt."

Ellen rubbed her thumb along the ceramic ridge of her mug and thought of the boulder that had slammed into the ground like a period at the end of a threat. How could a ghost have so much power? Most of them could barely tap on a flashlight or slide the planchette across the Ouija board.

"Read the part about the trap that killed him," she said softly. "Even if we know how it ends."

Sue reopened the book and turned a few pages back to the chapter that followed Louisa's—the one where the world exacts its price. "It's similar to what we watched in Jason's video summaries," she said. "Foster's wife. The soldier feigning sickness. The attic. The poker."

She read a paragraph that recast the scene—the clatter of cutlery, the smell of stew, the pistol laid on a table like an extra place setting. Bolin's suspicion, then loosening. The sound above. The threat. The false weakness on the stairs.

"February first, eighteenth sixty-two," Sue finished, "and he was twenty-one."

The heater hummed again; the building clicked. A neighbor's door opened and shut. In the little silences, the past seemed to lean closer, curious.

"Do you think he's angry about that?" Tanya asked. "About the trickery? The humiliation? Or just about being dead?"

"Yes," Ellen said simply. "All of it. And about Louisa. About promises that didn't survive her." She looked at the book in Sue's lap. "If the author's right—that Alf told himself he was protecting Missourians from outsiders—then anybody hunting his treasure is the worst kind of outsider. We're the very thing his story says to resist."

Sue stared into her mug. "Treasure or no, I want the house safe. I want to sleep there without feeling like I'm trespassing in my own kitchen."

"We'll make it safe," Ellen said.

Tanya readjusted the throw blanket over her legs, a defensive fort of fleece. "So, what's the plan? Talk to Louisa?"

The suggestion startled Ellen with its rightness. They'd gone to Murder Rocks reaching for men—James, Elijah, Sawyer—voices carved out of violence. A woman's voice might be easier to find. Or harder. Or truer.

"If she's there," Ellen said, careful of hope, "we can try. Maybe she has something to say."

Sue nodded. "Maybe she wants the story told right. If Sawyer is guarding the gold because he thinks it's sacred, maybe Louisa would tell him it's just metal. Or that what needs protecting isn't buried in a cave."

"Her memory," Tanya said. "Not his hoard."

They sat with that. The book waited between them like a fourth friend, taciturn but necessary.

Sue glanced down and skimmed. "There's a line here about Louisa being a spark," she said. "Not literally—it's not poetry—but a spark in the sense that she lit things. People. Causes. And after what happened, the fire just kept burning in a different direction."

Ellen thought of what fire does. It clears, it destroys, it feeds the ground with ash and asks new things to grow. But fire also makes the air sharp; it leaves you coughing. That had always been the trouble with haunted houses and haunted landscapes—you never knew if the past was fertile or poisonous. Usually both.

"Tell me something good about her," Ellen said. "Not just the tragedy. What did she love? Was there anything recorded?"

Sue's eyes softened as she searched. "There's a mention of her singing," she said, surprised. "Not like a performer—just that she had a habit of humming. Apparently, Alf wrote about it to his sister."

"That's something," Tanya said. "Ghosts like that. Small domestic details. If she hummed, maybe there's a melody to follow."

Ellen closed her eyes and listened, half playacting, and half because the room asked for it. To her surprise, something like a tune rose up—a scrap of childhood nothing, a few notes repeated, then a song.

Frère Jacques, Frère Jacques,
Dormez-vous? Dormez-vous?
Sonnez les matines! Sonnez les matines!

Ding, dang, dong. Ding, dang, dong.

When she opened her eyes, Sue and Tanya were watching her like she'd reached across a table and touched their hands without meaning to.

"We don't have to go tonight," Tanya said quickly, as if she'd sensed which direction the room was tilting. "We can try tomorrow, in daylight. I'd like to be able to see what tries to kill me."

"That would be a change," Sue said, winning a reluctant smile from both of them.

Ellen nodded. "Tomorrow," she agreed. "We'll bring something for Louisa. A ribbon? Something red."

"A ribbon's good," Sue said. "Red seems right."

"Oh, how about the silk ribbon from our gift basket?" Tanya crossed to the kitchen and pulled the ribbon from the basket of teas and coffees the condo manager had left for them. As she returned to the sofa with the ribbon in hand, she added, "If we're bribing a ghost, we should do it properly."

They let themselves laugh at that—gently, not because anything was funny, but because the living need to hear themselves sound alive in rooms where the dead are being discussed.

Tanya blew on her tea until the steam curled like a cat's tail, then took a sip. "All right. Tomorrow we'll reach out to Louisa. But for now, I'm going to pretend this is a normal girls' trip and watch something stupid before bed."

"Stupider than a haunted outlaw train robbery?" Sue asked.

"Much stupider," Tanya said. "Bake-off stupid."

Ellen smiled. The tilt of the evening righted a little. She took the book from Sue, found where they had left off, and placed a sticky note between the pages as a temporary bookmark. When she closed the cover, the apartment seemed to exhale with them.

Through the patio doors, Branson's night shrugged glitter over the hills. The light from a distant Ferris wheel turned red, then blue, then white, painting the glass in slow pulses. It was the sort of view that made everything seem festive whether you wanted it to be or not.

Ellen set the book on the coffee table and leaned back into the couch, her shoulder brushing Sue's. Tanya reached her foot out and tapped Ellen's ankle with her toe—softer than a nudge; more like a reminder that they were all still here.

CHAPTER TEN

Renovations and Resistance

Friday morning, frost silvered the grass along the gravel drive as Ellen eased the rental car to a stop. The Victorian's steep gables and turret towered overhead, but the new gray paint and royal blue trim made it appear less ominous, even friendly. A compressor thumped rhythmically somewhere inside, and classic rock bled faintly through an open window: a human soundtrack laid over a house that had its own music.

"Oh, wow," Sue said, unclicking her seat belt. "It looks amazing."

"They aren't wasting any time," Tanya put in.

Ellen shut her door and inhaled the crisp air. A blue jay chattered from an oak and scolded them, as if they were late.

"I can't wait to see how it's coming together on the inside," Sue said, leading the way up the porch steps.

The front door swung inward before she could knock. Caleb filled the doorway in a dusty hoodie and ballcap, utility knife clipped to his pocket. He managed a smile that looked like it had been ironed flat.

"Morning," he said. "You three got a minute?"

"That's why we're here," Sue said brightly, then faltered. "Is everything okay?"

Caleb stepped back to let them in. The entry still smelled like old wood, but there was a brightness to it now—fresh primer on the walls, taped edges crisp, floors covered with rosin paper and blue painter's tape marching along the baseboards like a tiny army. A radio sat on the hall table beside a box of finish nails. Somewhere toward the back, a nail gun popped twice.

"It's mostly okay," Caleb said, scrubbing a hand over his jaw. "But I won't lie: it's been a morning."

He led them into the parlor. The room already looked transformed—the wallpaper gone, the plaster skimmed, and a soft, Victorian-appropriate blue rolled onto the walls. The fireplace mantle, all carved scrolls and grape leaves, had been cleaned and oiled; the marble surround glowed.

"I had five guys here at eight," Caleb said. "*Had*. Now I have two."

Ellen's stomach dipped. "They quit?"

"Two of 'em did." He gestured toward the far wall. "And before you think they were being dramatic—well, maybe they were—but also, there's this."

He beckoned them closer. Ellen stepped around a drop cloth and came shoulder to shoulder with him, Sue and Tanya crowding in. At first she didn't see it—just the pearly sheen of the fresh paint and the faint orange-peel texture of the roller. Then the light from the tall window shifted, and it clicked into view: a pair of handprints, side by side, ghostly in white. Not greasy. Not grimy. Dusty-white on blue—as if hands dipped in flour had pressed there and lifted away, leaving only absence outlined by something finer than chalk.

Sue exhaled through her teeth. "What am I looking at?"

Tanya's fingers found the sleeve of Ellen's coat and pinched. "Tell me somebody did that as a joke."

Caleb shook his head. "Painter swears it showed up while he was down on the baseboard, cutting in. He stood up to reposition the ladder, looked over, and there they were. He yelled so loud my guy in the kitchen dropped a screwdriver."

Ellen leaned close. The prints weren't small—not a child's. The heel of each palm was crisp, and the finger lengths matched an adult male. But the thing that needled was the angle. Not casual. Not slap-and-go. The hands were braced there, as if someone had leaned in close to listen through the wall.

"Did you touch them?" she asked.

"I was going to wipe 'em," Caleb said. "Then the drawers tried to take my feet off."

"Pardon?" Sue said blankly.

"In the kitchen," he said, hooking a thumb toward the back of the house. "I was lifting the right-side cabinet—one of your uppers— onto the rail. Heavy sucker. If it comes down, it's not going back up without three guys and a prayer. My other guy is holding the bottom steady. Next thing you know, every drawer in the bank below us yanks open at once—hard. Like something kicked 'em from the inside. The top one whacked my shin; I nearly dropped the cabinet on my head and stepped off the ladder wrong. Twisted my ankle and said some words my mama would've washed out of my mouth."

Tanya winced in sympathy. "You okay?"

"I'll live. Pride hurts worse." He looked at Sue. "I told myself to be reasonable. New house, old bones—wood swells, slides. Air pressure from a door. Whatever. I would've written off the handprints, too, if it weren't for the timing. And the fact that the drawers don't just explode open by themselves."

"You sure the rails are level?" Sue asked, trying to give him a way out. "Sometimes those soft-close mechanisms fight you, don't they?"

"They fight you on the last two inches," Caleb said dryly. "They don't throw a punch."

Silence unspooled. The radio in the hall fizzed into a guitar riff and then faded as someone turned the volume down. A cold draft skated along Ellen's neck, near the scratches from the other day. She wanted to say it was the door, the window, the season—but the house felt watchful, like a cat with its ears forward.

"Two of my guys quit," Caleb repeated, words scraping. "Good men. One of them's got a baby on the way. He's spooked. The other— honestly, he just doesn't like feeling like a fool. I can't pay them enough to work scared."

"What about the third guy who left?" Ellen asked.

"He said he needed the weekend to think about it."

"Are you quitting?" Sue asked, voice small in a way that made Ellen look at her, startled. Sue rarely sounded small.

Caleb lifted both hands, then dropped them. "That's the thing. I don't want to. Your job's a good job. It's honest work. And I like making old things better. But I also can't keep guys if they think the cabinets are gonna attack them."

Tanya folded her arms tight, as if hugging herself. "We're so sorry," she said, earnest, cheeks pink with apology she couldn't possibly owe. "We should have warned you. We thought the cleansing helped."

"It probably did," Caleb said. "Until it didn't."

Ellen stepped closer to the handprints and put her palm up beside one, not touching it. "We can fix this," she said, surprising herself with the solidity in her voice. "We can make it better."

"How?" Caleb asked, and Ellen heard more than skepticism. He wanted a reason to stay.

"By cleansing the house again," Sue said, finding her footing. "Top to bottom. We'll sage and salt and splash holy water and say words that make even stubborn things flinch."

Ellen nodded. "We'll command anything negative to go."

Caleb squinted at them, not unkind. "Command, huh?"

Sue offered him a small smile. "We're bossy when we have to be."

He huffed, not quite laughter, but a truce. "Look. I'll be straight. I'm embarrassed even bringing this up. Painters talk. Carpenters talk. I don't want to be the guy complaining the drawers are possessed. But I don't want to see anyone get hurt, either. Including me."

"Don't quit," Sue said. "Please. We'll handle the house guests. We work fast."

"We can also sweeten the deal," Ellen added, glancing at Sue. Sue nodded minutely.

"Another two thousand," Sue said, as calmly as if she were offering him a bottle of water. "For the hassle. For lost time. For bravery."

Caleb blinked. "You don't have to—"

"I know," Sue said. "I want to."

He stared at the handprints another beat, jaw working. Then he gave a tight nod. "Okay. I'll keep the crew on—for now. But I want my guys outside while you do . . . you know."

"Exorcise the cabinets?" Ellen suggested.

"Hey, if the shoe fits," Caleb said. His shoulders dropped a fraction. "I'll send the last men out now. We'll take an early break."

He stuck his head into the hall and whistled. "Twenty minutes, smoke 'em if you got 'em," he called.

The two crewmen—bearded, mid-thirties, one thin, one round—ducked out of the kitchen with relief and followed Caleb onto the porch. The radio clicked off. The compressor shuddered to a stop. Quiet swelled.

Sue turned to Ellen and Tanya. "Let's gear up."

They set their bags on the parlor floor and began the ritual of unpacking: bundles of sage wrapped with thread; a small ceramic bowl for catching ash; a lighter; a screw-top jar of salt; a spray bottle of holy water Ellen always carried in her purse.

"Start at the top?" Tanya asked.

"Front to back, bottom to top," Ellen said. "Let's make some noise."

Sue opened a window. "Noise?" she asked.

"Things that cling don't love clang," Ellen said. "Ask any pan drawer." She grabbed a metal paint roller pole from a corner and banged it lightly on the threshold. The sound rang like a tuning fork. "Like Father Yamamoto's bell."

Tanya lit the sage. The first tendrils of smoke rose straight, then curled, sweet and bitter all at once. "All right," she said softly, more to the house than to her friends. "I'm ready."

They worked the parlor first. Sue carried the bowl beneath the smoldering bundle as Tanya wafted smoke into corners, around window casings, over the mantle. Ellen followed with her spray bottle, flicking mist along baseboards, dropping a pinch of salt into each corner where shadow pooled. The handprints seemed to pale as the air thickened, or maybe that was wishful thinking. Either way, Ellen refused to test whether they wiped off.

"Our intention," she said aloud, steadying her breath. "This is a home for the living, a place of work, a place of rest. Any energy that means harm must leave. Any energy that thinks it owns this place is mistaken. You are commanded to go—out the doors, out the windows, out the cracks—go to the trees where you belong, or to the river, or to the road. But not here."

Tanya added, "We acknowledge your pain, your anger, your fear. But this house is not a stage for it." She glanced at Ellen. "How am I doing?"

"Ferocious," Ellen said, and meant it.

They moved to the dining room, then the hallway. At the back stairs, Tanya paused, eyes tracking upward like a cat's. "Feels weird here."

"Back stairs always do," Ellen said.

They climbed. On the landing, the air felt subtly cooler, the way a room feels after someone has left in a hurry. Tanya smoke-traced the risers; Sue salted the corners; Ellen misted the wall beside the banister, the spray fine enough to turn the winter light into glitter for a second before it fell.

Upstairs, they did the turret bathroom, the bedrooms, the long hallway with its runner rolled back and its nail heads glinting along the floor like braille. In the room where Jason Albright had died, they slowed, breath lining up without having to be asked. The new glass that had recently been installed glinted in the sunlight; the sash was whole again. But blue tape still crossed the corners like a bandage.

"Here," Sue whispered.

They stood in a triangle around the center of the room. Tanya's hand shook just enough to make the sage ember brighten and fall in a red fleck into the bowl. Ellen felt the cold lift the hairs along her forearms.

"Do no harm," Ellen said to the air. "Alf, Sawyer, Louisa? If you're here to cause trouble, consider these your marching orders."

The new window rattled in its frame. The three friends exchanged worried glances.

Bravely, Sue crossed the room and opened it. "Negative energy, we command you to leave this place, never to return."

Ellen misted the room while Tanya salted the corners.

By the time they'd finished the upstairs, Ellen's eyes stung, and her throat had that old incense ache. They went down the front stairs—Ellen brushing her fingers along the banister the way a person pats a horse—and crossed through rooms to the kitchen at the back of the house.

The new lower cabinets looked crisp and straight, their gray paint the kind of color that changed with the light—warmer in some, cooler in others. The drawers in question were all shut now, lined up like soldiers. The space where the last overhead cabinet would hang gaped patiently, bracket ready.

"Be nice," Sue told the bank of drawers, pointing at them with the sage like a scolding aunt. "We are not doing jump scares today."

Ellen snorted despite herself as Sue flicked salt into the toe-kick recesses, and Ellen spritzed a fine mist along the rail where the upper would mount.

They finished in the powder room beneath the back stairs and then returned to the parlor. Tanya crumbled the remaining sage into the bowl, eyes glassy from smoke. Sue fanned toward the open window with a piece of cardboard until the air felt lighter.

"Moment of truth," Ellen murmured.

They went to the porch. Caleb and his crewman were sitting on the steps drinking coffee from Styrofoam cups, breath visible in the cold. Caleb stood when he saw them, tamping down worry.

"All set?" he asked.

"Yes, we are," Sue assured him. "We stirred things and told them where to go."

Caleb toed at a knot in the porch board. "Do I want to know where?"

"Out," Ellen said succinctly.

"Fair." He opened the door. "We'll get back to it."

Inside, the compressor coughed back to life again, ending the lingering sense of disquiet. Ellen exhaled, only then realizing she'd been holding her breath like a fragile thing.

"Caleb?" Sue said, as he headed toward the kitchen. He looked over his shoulder at her to listen. "If anything else happens—if you see or hear or feel anything—call me. I don't care what time it is. Just keep us in the loop."

He nodded, relief erasing the lines around his eyes. "You got it."

"And ice that ankle," Sue added. "You pretending you're fine doesn't impress anyone."

Caleb grinned. "Noted."

As he disappeared into the kitchen, the radio clicked back on, braver this time, and someone laughed at something the deejay said. Ellen stood still one extra beat in the entry, listening to ordinary noises—a tape roll pulling, a hammer tapping, a man humming under his breath. The house seemed to tolerate it, if not exactly enjoy it.

"What now?" Tanya asked, low.

"Library," Ellen said. "We promised ourselves we'd track down those letters."

"And lunch," Sue said. "Research is hungry work."

Ellen smiled. "Deal."

They gathered their bags and stepped back into the cold, the air outside scouring their lungs clean. As they reached the car, Ellen glanced back. The affronted blue jay had claimed a high branch and watched them go, head cocked, bright and suspicious. Behind it, the Victorian's windows seemed to hold on to a little of the warmth they'd put into the rooms, like breath on glass.

"Stay that way," she whispered, not sure whether she meant the house or herself.

CHAPTER ELEVEN

Whispering Stacks

The Branson library was a low, modern building trimmed with stone, all warm glass and tidy landscaping. Inside, the air smelled like paper and citrus cleaner, and a dozen Christmas cutouts dangled from strings over the circulation desk. A young woman in a reindeer sweater worked a puzzle with a toddler at a nearby table while an older man in a camo cap read the newspaper as if it were still the primary engine of the world.

Ellen felt her shoulders loosen. Libraries did that to her—temples of order and possibility. Even when the stacks held horrors, they put them in call-number order.

They approached the reference desk where a young woman with a name tag that read "Maya" tapped at a keyboard with a speed that made Ellen want to applaud. Maya smiled as they came up.

"My daughter-in-law's name is Maya," Ellen said by way of greeting, feeling a momentary tug at her heart, a nostalgia for her kids.

"Hi." The librarian's eyes flicked up at them and then down again to her computer screen. "Can I help you find something?"

"We're looking for letters," Ellen said, realizing as she said it how ridiculous it sounded to ask for letters the way you might ask for sugar. She tried again. "Historical ones. From—possibly—from a man named Alf Bolin. Civil War era? We found a footnote about them, and we're trying to follow the crumbs."

Maya perked up like a retriever catching the word *walk*. "Civil War primary sources?" she said. "Fun."

"Your definition of fun and mine are the same," Sue muttered, earning a side-grin from Ellen.

Maya had already spun her screen toward a database. "Let's try the regional archives index first," she said, fingers dancing. She typed *Bolin, Alf* and then added *letters* and *Ozarks*. Her brow furrowed in pleased concentration.

The computer thought. Ellen held her breath as if her lungs were ballast and the screen a scale. Tanya hovered with her hands tucked into her coat pockets despite the warmth, as if she were afraid the information might bite.

"Huh," Maya said, and Ellen's heart flip-kicked. "We don't have them here, but . . . give me a second." More typing, a soft murmur that sounded like *come on, come on.* "Okay. I'm seeing an academic footnote in a journal article—hang on, let me pull just that part."

She squinted at the screen, then turned it so they could see while she read. "It says: *'Correspondence attributed to Alfred Bolin (ca. 1856– 1862), letters held by Oakdale School for the Blind, Springfield, Missouri, Special Collections.'*"

"Springfield," Sue repeated. She'd already pulled out her phone. "That's only forty-five minutes from here."

Maya clicked two more times and then a link opened to the journal listing. "There's no digitized scan here," she said apologetically. "But this is a good breadcrumb. If Oakdale has a special collections room, they'll have a librarian you can email or call. Sometimes schools with small archives are happy to let researchers in by appointment."

"Do we count as researchers?" Tanya asked Ellen and Sue.

Sue put her hands on her hips, warrior-ready. "Today we do."

Maya scribbled the citation on a sticky note with a candy-cane pen and handed it over. "Here. I'll also email you the link if you want."

"Please," Ellen said, writing her email on another sticky note. "You've been amazing."

"Just doing my favorite part of the job," Maya said. "Chasing ghosts." Then she flushed. "I mean—um—history ghosts."

"You're not wrong either way," Tanya said.

They thanked her again and drifted toward the exit, pausing only long enough for Ellen to run a hand down a shelf of Missouri histories and for Sue to admire a display of gingerbread house winners. Outside, the sun had pulled on a soft veil of cloud, and the parking lot had lessened its glare.

They climbed back into the Chevy, the interior still holding their morning heat. Sue was already map-hunting.

"Oakdale School for the Blind," she said from the back seat, thumbs zipping. "Springfield, south side. They do K through 12, but they've got a historic building with a small museum."

"Do they allow visitors?" Tanya asked.

"There's a phone number for the archivist," Sue said, triumphant. "A Ms. Loring. I can call now and see if they're open for a drop-in."

Sue put the call on speaker. After three rings, a warm voice answered, "Oakdale archives, this is Ms. Loring."

"Hi, Ms. Loring," Sue said, instantly charming. "We're researchers—informal ones—looking into Civil War correspondence attributed to Alf Bolin. A footnote pointed us to you. We're in Branson today and wondered whether it might be possible to make an appointment to view the letters."

There was a pause on the other end, as if the woman were rearranging mental files. "We do have letters attributed to an Alf Bolin—yes," she said slowly. "We don't have weekend hours for the archive, but you can come today if you can be here before noon. Otherwise, it'll have to wait until Monday."

"We can be there in forty-five minutes," Sue said, glancing at Ellen in the rearview mirror.

Ellen nodded, already angling the car from the parking lot.

"Bring clean hands," Ms. Loring said. "No pens. And your curiosity."

"We have that in abundance," Ellen said, leaning toward the phone. "Thank you."

"Door on the north side of the old building," Ms. Loring said. "I'll put my name on a note."

The call ended. The three of them looked at one another, grins lifting like kites.

"Road trip?" Ellen asked, eyebrows up.

"Road trip," Tanya echoed, bracing a hand on the dash as Ellen pulled out.

"I'll search up restaurants in Springfield," Sue said from the back, already scrolling. "There's a place with chicken and noodles that looks like it could cure generational trauma."

"Research fuel," Ellen said, feeling something bright unfurl in her chest. Sage smoke and salt and holy water were one way to push back. But sometimes the most powerful dispersal was knowledge—on paper, in names, in lines written by long-dead hands that refused to be quiet. Sometimes the best weapon was a library with an archivist.

They turned onto the highway, the hills shouldering up around them, winter-bare and honest. The Victorian would be there when they returned, its walls hopefully staying still, its drawers behaving, its paint drying without fingerprints forming like breath on a mirror. And in Springfield, the letters would hopefully add a spine to the story of Alf Bolin.

"If we're lucky, we can figure out what's motivating our ghost," Ellen said as she changed lanes.

"I like the way you think," Sue chimed in from the back.

Ellen laughed and pressed her foot a little more firmly to the gas. The car surged, the day widened, and ahead, the road bent toward answers.

The Oakdale School for the Blind sat back from the road behind a sweep of old oaks, its original brick building wearing a dignified patina that made Ellen think of bell choirs and chalk dust. Inside, the foyer smelled faintly of lemon oil and books. A glass case displayed braille slates, styluses, and photographs of students from the 1920s smiling with chins tilted toward the light. Somewhere down the corridor, someone practiced scales on a piano in a warm, halting loop.

"Archives are this way," said the woman who'd introduced herself on the phone as Ms. Loring. She was mid-fifties and wearing a charcoal cardigan with an enamel cardinal pin. Her voice carried the practiced calm of someone who spends her days coaxing stories out of paper. "We don't have much space, but what we keep, we keep properly."

She led them past a door marked "Special Collections" into a room that was both sparse and reverent: high windows, a long wooden table with three chairs, a coat tree, and a single museum case with a model of the campus. The only sounds were the sigh of the HVAC and the soft squeak of her sensible shoes.

"Set your bags there," she said, pointing to a shelf beneath a sign that read "NO FOOD OR DRINK!"

"Phones on silent, please. We'll use gloves." She smiled apologetically. "I know some institutions prefer clean hands over gloves for fragile paper, but these have soot residue and iron gall ink. The gloves keep you safe, too."

She unlocked a metal cabinet with a key on a ribbon around her neck and pulled out a gray archival box sealed with a strip of linen tape. She brought it to the table like a communion offering.

Ellen felt her breath slow down. The neatness of it—the procedure—always steadied her. You asked; you waited; you were granted. It was a kind of sacred courtesy.

"Our school considers these letters a great treasure," Ms. Loring said, setting the box down. "Annabel Bolin was a student here from 1856 to 1879, the year in which she died. Her brother wrote to her until just before his death in February of 1863. When Annabel passed, she had no living relatives to send her personal effects to, so the school kept these letters, due to her brother's infamy, and donated the rest."

Ms. Loring broke the tape, lifted the lid, and revealed a sealed polyethylene pouch, inside which was a stack of yellowed sheets folded into thirds, edges soft from existing for a century and a half. The black ink had browned in places but still lay sharp on the page.

"Gloves," Ms. Loring said, distributing three pairs of white cotton. "I'll open the pouch. You may handle one letter at a time. Support the page. No pens—only this pencil, if you must take notes." She set a yellow pencil and a trio of foam wedges on the table. "And a magnifier," she added, placing a handheld glass the size of a biscuit within easy reach.

Ellen slid her hands into the gloves, feeling like a child playing dress-up. The cotton dulled her fingerprints. Sue flexed her fingers and wiggled her eyebrows as if to say *look at us, professionals*. Tanya solemnly tugged her gloves tight like a surgeon.

Ms. Loring slit the pouch with a careful letter opener. She lifted the stack, squared it against her palm, and set the first sheet on a foam wedge.

"Every letter here is addressed to *Annabel*," she said, tapping the salutation with a gloved fingertip. "The dates run August 26, 1856 to December 12, 1862. Start where you like. I'll be at my desk if you need anything."

She retreated to a small desk by the door and began quietly tapping on her computer keyboard, a guardian angel within earshot.

Ellen swallowed and leaned in. The handwriting surprised her: steady, modest loops, the descenders neat, the capitals old-fashioned but not florid. A boy taught by a patient hand, she thought. The script had a rhythm, a kind of marching measure. The magnifying glass made the lines swell and then settle back into crispness.

"Ready?" Ellen asked, glancing at her friends.

Sue nodded, eyes bright.

Tanya said, "Hit me," then softened. "Sorry. Talk to me."

Ellen took up the magnifying glass and began.

August 26, 1856

Dear Annabel,

I find myself with a roof and a table and the good fortune of folks who call me by my proper name. After the Bilyeus—God keep them—I never thought I would feel beholden to anyone again, but Mary and Calvin Cloud are the kindest you'd ever met. They took me in though I told them I was fifteen and could get by on my own. Calvin laughed and said even a fifteen-year-old mule gets stuck in the mud. He says I can rub a horse down proper, and Mary says I eat with a fork like a gentleman and that is worth room and board.

They are wrong about only one thing and that is Negroes. They hold that Negroes have souls the same as any white man, and I cannot bring myself to believe it, for then everything we are fighting for would be for nothing. Mary says God made them and so they have souls. I say God made mules, too, and mules are strong but no more Christian than a stump. We do not quarrel. We eat and bow our heads, and I help Calvin mend fences, and I say my piece to you instead of to them.

There is a teacher here, Miss Fulton. I didn't think I'd like school, but the Clouds insisted. Miss Fulton makes us read Shakespeare. There is a sonnet: "Love is not love / Which alters when it alteration finds." I think about it a great deal.

That sonnet is Mary-Ann Cox's favorite. She smiles when I say it, and I would say it wrong on purpose for her to correct me. One day I will wed Mary-Ann, and I will bring her to you. You will like her.

Your brother, Alf

Ellen paused. A quiet passed over the table: not solemn, exactly, but attentive, the way a room leans when someone is about to confess a secret.

"He was a baby," Tanya murmured. "Talking like a man, but he was a baby."

"The bit about souls," Sue said, grimacing. "How disturbing."

Ellen traced the air beside the sonnet line, not touching the ink. "Miss Fulton planted something positive," she said. "Even if it didn't bloom."

They traded a look—acknowledging the complicated, the human—then Sue eased the next letter onto the wedge. Taking up the magnifying glass, Sue cleared her throat and read, adopting a light, wry cadence that softened the sharper edges of the text:

October 20, 1856

Dear Annabel,

Miss Fulton refuses to speak of politics in the schoolroom. I asked her plain if she thought Negroes should be free, and she set her jaw and said, 'In this classroom, we leave today's world outside. We are discussing history, Alf.' I told her we cannot avoid talking of it forever. It is upon us like weather. I asked what she thought of Douglas's bill, and she folded her hands and told me to fetch my book. She would not be moved, not even by me.

Calvin says a man's work is to tend what is his to tend. I do not know what is mine, only that something is stirring and I cannot sit and watch it pass.

Your brother, Alf

"'Weather,'" Ellen said, impressed and irritated at once. "He sees the storm and thinks he's meant to be lightning."

They shared a brief frown, then Tanya eased the third letter free. Her gloved fingers were careful, her mouth set; holding up the magnifying glass, she read with a steadier cadence than usual, as if honoring an oath.

November 28, 1856

Dear Annabel,

I had dinner with Mary-Ann's parents because I meant to ask for her hand in marriage. Her father, Mr. Mervin Cox, says he supports the right to own slaves, and I told him I do as well. Her mother, Mrs. Cox, said that a person cannot be owned and to do so was to commit a mortal sin.

Mary-Ann cannot make up her mind about slavery. She says she wants to read more and then decide. Mr. Cox says this is a bad time to marry, and he is sending Mary-Ann to a girls' school in California. I told her we should run away. She said she wants to go to school. I said I would go with her, that Romeo and Juliet were younger than us and they did not ask permission. She laughed and said that was not the argument I thought it was, and that there are endings and then there are endings. She says this is something she must do alone.

I do not like being told to wait. I feel like a horse tied to a post when the barn is on fire.

I hope to visit you at Christmas.

Your brother, Alf

The room seemed to tilt slightly, the past shifting like a sleeper turning over. Ellen saw the shape of the boy more clearly: prideful and tender, hungry for a path that would bless the heat inside him.

"California," Tanya breathed. "Twenty-first century me wants to DM Mary-Ann: You go, girl."

"She went," Sue pointed out. "Alone. Which makes room for Louisa."

All three looked down at the stack as if the next sheet might burn before they lifted it. Ellen slid out the fourth letter. The date jumped: January 3, 1857 had been scrawled at the top, then scratched out, then rewritten more carefully as February 3, 1857—the ink darker there, the correction human.

Through the glass, Ellen read, the words shaping themselves in her throat:

February 3, 1857

Dear Annabel,

The Bilyeu's niece came to live with us. Her name is Louisa O'Hare, and you would like her. She is as fiery as her red hair, which is curly and long and thick. When she pins it up, she is as tall as me, and I am six feet. Her parents—Dad Bilyeus's sister and brother-in-law—were killed and her home destroyed by abolitionists. The fire that burned her farm is still burning, and I can see it. She despises the North as much as me.

She says we are fighters as we are able-bodied citizens of the South, and we should do what we can for the cause. She says she will go with or without me. I said we would need horses, and she grinned and kissed me full on the mouth, and I forgot what I was going to say. I think I am falling in love again, Annabel. Louisa is mending my broken heart.

I will bring her to you if I can keep up with her.

Your brother, Alf

Sue's hand had crept over the table toward the page, hovering there as if to feel the heat of it. "There she is," she whispered. "The spark."

Tanya swallowed. "The tinder was already stacked."

Ellen stared at the line about the kiss, the way the ink had deepened over *forgot*. You could feel the skid of the pen, the rush of the boy. She imagined Louisa's laugh, a whip crack and a bell.

"Next," Sue said softly, and pulled the fifth letter free.

April 9, 1857

Dear Annabel,

Louisa convinced me that we should requisition horses, saying it was in service of the South. I told her we could get shot for being thieves, and she said we would not be thieves because we would bring them back when we had used them for good, and also we should wait until dark because she is not a fool.

We watched a lanky man in his thirties lead two horses into a barn. We waited until he went back to the house. When we slipped inside, a lantern flared, and a Colt revolver was pointed at my head. Louisa said, "We are requisitioning these horses." The man asked, "For what?" I did not know if he was Union or Southern and my mouth would not decide what to say. Louisa said, "We are in the service of the South. If you are a Unionist, you might as well kill us now. We will have died with honor."

The man laughed and lowered the gun and said his name was Robert Foster. He said he did not like brave children dying in his barn. He invited us to meet his wife and stay for dinner. Mrs. Grace Foster made a sweet meat dish and fried potatoes with onions, the best food I have ever tasted. They asked questions and did not push. They gave us a bed for the night and in the morning, they said they would not give us horses, but they gave us two guns, a sack of deer jerky, and a map to Gamble Farm, where men were training horses for the Union. He said we could start by stealing horses and information from the Unionists. He would send other men to help with word of where to go from there.

Your brother, Alf

The name Foster landed like a small stone dropped into a still pond—ripples widening toward a death Ellen already knew. She felt Tanya's gaze meet hers, both of them thinking ahead to a dinner table, to a pistol laid beside a plate like an extra utensil, to a poker lifted by an executioner.

"Same Fosters?" Tanya breathed.

"Has to be," Ellen said.

They sat back, each of them taking turns with the magnifier, reading again in silence, tracing letters without touching them, running the words through different filters—boy, lover, soldier, outlaw—like holding a photograph to the light to watch another picture rise behind it.

At the desk, Ms. Loring glanced up once, as if sensing the shift in the air, then returned to her computer monitor. The radiator clinked. A janitor's cart rolled past far down the hall and squeaked again into quiet.

Ellen felt hunger creep in at the edges of her attention—first as a faint irritation, then as a hollow yawning. She ignored it until Tanya's stomach undercut her restraint with a theatrical growl that vibrated the table's wood.

All three froze, then dissolved into muffled laughter, the sound disarming and necessary.

"I'm so sorry," Tanya whispered, folding an arm over her midsection as if to muffle the traitor within.

Sue checked the clock on the wall. "We've been here for over an hour." She lowered her voice. "Ask if we can come back after lunch?"

Ellen stood and walked to the desk. "Ms. Loring?"

The archivist looked up, eyes kind behind rectangular frames. "How is it?"

"Like finding a voice in a room we thought was empty," Ellen said truthfully. "Would it be possible to take a quick lunch and return?"

A shadow of regret passed over Ms. Loring's face. "I'm afraid not. We close the archives in thirty minutes. It's just me, and I've got to be at the front for a student exhibit set-up." She paused, then brightened. "However, if you can't return on Monday, I can scan what you haven't read—at least up to a dozen letters. Our flatbed is gentle. I'll have to do it myself, given the condition, but I'm happy to email you PDFs before the end of the day."

"That would be incredible," Ellen said, meaning it more than the phrase usually carried. "We're deeply grateful."

"Mark the ones you want most," Ms. Loring said, reaching for a pad of miniature sticky flags. "I'll prioritize those, then work through the rest as time allows."

Back at the table, Ellen relayed the plan. Sue's face lit up. Tanya exhaled a sigh that sounded suspiciously like *pie*.

They skimmed through the remaining letters and chose eleven that referred to Louisa, Sawyer, and, later, to Alf's gang of Merry Men.

"Let's definitely flag the last letter," Ellen added. "I want to know where his head was on December 12, 1862."

They handled the stack again with reverence. The last envelope Ellen slid free did indeed carry that winter date. She pressed the flag to it like a promise.

"All right," she said softly to the paper, to the room, to the boy in the ink. "We'll be back, one way or another."

They returned their gloves to a small basket, took one last look at the neatness of the table, and thanked Ms. Loring again.

"Clean hands, full hearts, careful minds," the archivist said, smiling them out like a benediction. "I'll email you before supper."

In the hall, Ellen felt the press of the building's history—blind students learning to read the world with their fingers, teachers counting steps between desks, the steady mercy of systems that help humans find what they need. She thought of the letters crossing time, of ink that outlived breath.

Outside, the light had softened to a tender gray. Their breath made small clouds.

Sue slid her hands into her coat pockets and bounced on her toes. "I looked up a chicken-and-noodles place," she said. "Also a pie shop. We could do both. For research."

"Protein, then sugar," Tanya said, dead serious. "Like an exorcism for my stomach."

Ellen laughed, the sound loosening something that had wound tight around her ribs. "Let's feed the living," she said, unlocking the car. "Then we'll let a dead boy talk some more."

As they pulled out of the lot, Ellen glanced back at the brick building with its quiet windows and pictured Ms. Loring leaning over the scanner, each page flattening under the gentle lid, the light bar passing and catching up every pen stroke. A different kind of séance, she thought. The kind with gloves and pencils and someone saying *I'll be at my desk if you need me.*

Beside her, Tanya's eyes were already closed in a pre-lunch nap. In the rearview, Sue scrolled through her phone, humming under her breath. Ellen turned onto the road, the city opening like another book. The past would be waiting in her inbox by evening, and for once, the dead felt almost cooperative.

"Chicken and noodles," Sue announced, triumphant. "Then pie as big as your head."

"Annabel would approve," Tanya said, eyes still closed.

"Annabel," Ellen echoed, testing the name. She didn't know why it felt like a key, only that it did. The syllables settled in her mouth and made a small, stubborn home there.

They drove toward lunch and whatever came after, the letters' voices riding along with them like passengers who, for now, chose to keep their hands to themselves.

CHAPTER TWELVE

The Man at Murder Rocks

By the time they turned off JJ Highway onto the gravel lane, the light had softened into that late-winter gold that made every bare branch look edged in brass. Ellen felt the drive's familiar jounce under the tires, the Victorian's turret rising ahead like a chess piece. After the hush of the archives and the soothing monotony of Springfield traffic, the house looked friendly—its porch a wide yawn, its windows reflecting the pale sky.

Caleb's pickup and a white cargo van sat side by side near the carport. As Ellen parked, she could hear the compressor's steady thrum and the knock-tap of a hammer. Work sounds. Normalcy.

Inside, the house met them with the smell of wet paint and cut pine. Blue painter's tape ran like neat veins along the baseboards; a roller tray gleamed with fresh eggshell. Somewhere toward the kitchen, a cordless drill whirred and sputtered.

Caleb appeared in the hall wiping his hands on a rag, ballcap shoved backward, a length of pencil tucked above one ear. He grinned, real and relieved.

"Ladies," he said. "No more theatrics since this morning."

"None?" Sue asked, hopeful and wary all at once.

"None," he said, holding up a hand as if swearing it on a Bible. "No surprise handprints. No kamikaze drawers. If something's still here, it's keeping to itself."

"Oh, what a relief," Ellen said with a sigh.

Caleb rocked on his heels. "Your cleansing tour must've done something. One of the guys even said the place felt lighter. He also might be angling for a raise."

"You'll get a bonus when we're done," Sue said. "Thank you for sticking with us."

"Thanks for not thinking I'm crazy," Caleb said, then flicked his eyes to Ellen. "You going to head back out to the rocks today?"

Ellen smiled at him, impressed as always by how quickly the practical-minded adjusted to their oddities. "We are," she said. "With caution."

"Good," he said. "I'll keep my phone nearby in case you need help—or if I need a priest."

They traded grins. Then Caleb melted back toward the kitchen, his voice floating ahead of him as he told someone to ease up on the nail gun. Ellen lingered in the hall for a moment, listening—men working, the house accepting it. Maybe their smoke and salt and stern words had actually shifted the room's posture.

"Ready?" Sue said, as she headed for the door. "Before it gets dark?"

"Let's go meet a ghost," Tanya said, not sounding thrilled about it but sounding game.

They grabbed their gear from the trunk: Ellen's SLS camera and EMF meter; the spirit box and external speaker; one tripod with a quick-release plate; two handheld full-spectrum cameras (one for Sue, one in case they needed backup); Tanya's EVP recorder and shotgun microphone; headlamps; a coil of extra batteries; a zippered pouch with spare SD cards. Ellen checked the spirit box's battery level, then stuffed a water bottle into her bag.

They took the back path that dropped down the hill. The afternoon had cooled; the leaf litter crackled underfoot, a thousand tiny exclamations. The slope here was steep enough to make Ellen plant each foot carefully—dry oak leaves over clay made treachery of even small inclines. The air smelled of damp rock and something green surviving the winter.

The trees thinned as they neared the first limestone outcrops. Murder Rocks lived up to their name in texture if not intent—great hunched forms like the backs of sleeping beasts, pocked with shallow caves and scooped-out shelves. In the alcoves, the air was a few degrees colder, the kind that licked old injuries. Ellen knew from experience how sound behaved down here—how a footstep could echo wrong, how a voice could ricochet and come back sounding a half-inch off, like a copy of itself.

They chose a shelf that gave them a decent view of the funnel-shaped gully below and a jag of rock rising like a rostrum. Ellen kicked away a half-rotted branch, cleared a patch of ground with her heel, and set the tripod. She mounted the camera, checked the level, then framed the shot to take in the rock face, the gully, and the faint suggestion of the path beyond.

"Rolling," she said, tapping record. The camera's red light winked alive.

Sue flipped her full-spectrum camera on and tested the zoom. "Alive on B cam."

Tanya pulled the thin, silk ribbon from her bag and laid it next to the tripod, a sliver of bright red popping against gray rock and brown dirt and dead leaves. Then, she looped her headphones over her ears, connected the EVP recorder to the shotgun mic, and extended the mic's shock mount with a small flourish. "I'm ready," she said, tilting the mic toward the open air. "I feel like a weather reporter," she added under her breath.

Ellen set the spirit box on the flat of a wide, waist-high rock and synced the small external speaker so they wouldn't have to huddle. The box's display flickered, then settled. She set the sweep to medium-fast; she preferred that metallic staccato, the way it forced voices to work for audibility. The EMF meter she clipped to her jacket pocket, its single LED bar dark.

They took a beat and just stood there, listening. Birds muttered; a branch clicked as it shifted; the highway far below hissed like distant surf. The whole hollow seemed to hold its breath the way a chapel does when someone steps to the pulpit.

"All right," Sue said softly, projecting without shouting. "I'm Sue. These are my friends, Ellen and Tanya. We're back. We mean no harm. We're here to tell stories right and to make a house safe for the living."

Ellen watched the band of trees across the gully as she always did in the first few minutes—waiting for anything that wasn't wind. She also watched the SLS screen, the algorithm's little green lines ready to snap into a human-shaped stick figure if the software perceived the right pattern of angles.

"We'd like to speak to Louisa O'Hare," Sue continued, voice steady. "Fighter for the South. Friend of Alf Bolin."

The spirit box filled the clearing with its indifferent chatter—syllables shredded by the sweep, bits of music sliced to confetti, static popping like fat in a pan. Ellen's brain did the thing it always did, trying to make meaning out of noise; her body did the other thing it always did, prickling with the sense that meaning was possible.

She did not expect a direct reply. Usually, the box was coy.

"This is Louisa," it said.

It wasn't the voice she would have chosen. It was genderless and granular, syllables snatched out of two adjacent stations and married long enough to be comprehensible. Still, the cadence was there: *This is Louisa.*

Sue's head whipped toward the box. Tanya's eyes went wide, then skeptical. Ellen's heart kicked against her ribs.

"It could be a trickster," Ellen said automatically, duty and experience making her play referee to her own hope.

"Let's verify," Tanya said, leaning in, mic aimed like an offering.

Ellen swallowed and asked the question she would have asked any unknown: "How old were you when you died?"

The box hissed and pulsed, the sweep clicking like the teeth of a comb. Then a number formed out of the chop, solid as a step: "Twenty-two."

Tanya's face tugged into that complicated shape it wore when fear and curiosity wrestled to a draw. Sue made a small sound—a cross between *ha* and *oh*.

"How did you die?" Sue asked, voice couched but strong.

Static. Then a stretch of two syllables that sounded a lot like "Secesh."

Tanya repeated the word with incredulity.

Ellen felt the hair stand at the nape of her neck, and she reached back to touch the scratches she'd received there the other night.

"We're so sorry, Louisa," Sue said softly to the air and to the rock and to the hollow that held them. "We read about you."

Ellen added, "We need your help."

On the SLS screen, a spiky outline sparked into existence at the edge of the rock shelf, not quite human yet—more like a spider's sketch of a person. Ellen held her breath and shifted the camera half an inch. The figure flickered, then stabilized into a stick—a tiny torso, arms a little too long, one leg bent at an odd angle the way occlusion sometimes made limbs do.

"I've got something," she whispered. "Small. Edge of the shelf."

Tanya angled her mic that way, eyes squeezed shut as if that sharpened her hearing. In Ellen's pocket, the EMF meter chirped—the first bar lifting to green. Ellen felt her mouth go dry.

"Do you know who killed Jason Albright?" Ellen asked. If there was a time to be blunt, it was now.

The box hissed, the sweep clicking. For a beat, Ellen thought the answer would be silence. Then the speakers spit one crisp syllable like a stone tossed into their circle: "Yes."

"Please tell us his or her name," Sue said quickly, before the air could close around them again. She leaned toward the rock as if it might help the spirit hear better from there.

A sound pressed through the slicer—a breath that became consonants: "Sawyer."

Ellen's pulse tripped over itself. She looked up at her friends, saw her own shock reflected back. "Did it say Sawyer?" The stick figure on her SLS shivered and then dissolved into nothing. The EMF bar fell to zero like a curtain drop.

"Yes, Sawyer," Tanya repeated, the name warping slightly in her mouth as if she didn't want it to fit there. "Was he protecting Alf's treasure?"

The box cackled—static rising in a tangled burble, a suggestion of a phrase like *bear claws*, and then a smear that could have been anything. The sweep hiccupped, as if it had lost purchase.

"Say that again," Ellen said, trying to coax. "Was Sawyer protecting the treasure? Yes or no."

The box stuttered. The sounds were unintelligible before collapsing into a blanket of silence.

Ellen was about to set the box to a different sweep speed when the woods spoke. A footfall. Then another. Not the gentle weight of a deer; not the blunt, communal shuffle of raccoons. Human. Or something that wanted to sound human.

She pivoted, scanning the slope above them. The path cut a diagonal along the hill; the leaf litter there was disturbed—fresh scuffs, a trail of crushed oak leaves like a cheap underline. A shape flitted between trunks—tallish, broad-shouldered, a dark shirt against the pale trees.

"Who's there?" she called, just loud enough to carry.

The figure jolted, then bolted uphill, a clatter of steps and sliding soil. For a half-second Ellen's brain filed it under *ghost*—habit and expectation doing their trick—until the runner tripped, windmilled, cussed, and caught himself with a very physical grunt.

Definitely not a ghost.

"Hey!" Ellen shouted, switching tack mid-breath. "Hello?"

The man paused at the next tree and turned. He was bald, pale, flushed, mid-forties maybe, and lean. He threw up a hand in a wave, sheepish.

"Sorry!" he called back. "Didn't mean to disturb your investigation!"

Sue swung her camera off him. "No worries," she called up, voice warm and steel-spined in equal measure. "Are you lost?"

He picked his way back down toward them, watching his feet. "No, ma'am," he said, breath hitching. "I heard this is public property now."

"Not yet," Sue said. She straightened, the queen of a small, haunted kingdom. "I haven't signed the paperwork yet. In a few months, yes."

He clicked his tongue, recalculating. "Oh. Are you the new owner?"

"Yes, sir, I am," Sue said. She kept her chin friendly and her gaze level. "I'm Sue Graham. These are my friends, Tanya and Ellen."

"Bill Kirby," he said, hesitating before offering the name as if he might need to swap it out later. He stayed two arm-lengths back from their equipment, eyes flicking from the tripod to the spirit box to the mic. "You, uh, do this a lot?"

"Often enough," Sue replied.

Tanya removed her headphones and gave Ellen a look of uneasiness.

"Have you been out here before, Mr. Kirby?" Ellen asked, letting curiosity wear the coat of politeness.

"A few times," he admitted. His gaze darted toward the mouth of one of the caves as if it might cough up a secret if he stared hard enough.

"Well," Sue said, allowing a sigh just the right side of theatrical, "for now, anyway, you're trespassing. Mind telling me why?"

He spread his hands, the universal gesture of *no gun, no threat.* "Just another treasure hunter looking for Bolin's stash. Didn't mean any harm. Like I said, I thought it was public. I'll—uh—I'll come back in a few months."

"I wouldn't bother," Sue said, smiling a smile that could have meant anything and everything. "Because I'll have found it before then."

Ellen hid her grin. Sue's eyes sparkled as if she'd just tossed a pebble into a pond to watch the ripples.

Bill Kirby didn't seem to know how to catch it. He laughed once, thin and high pitched; his face went a shade paler, then flushed. "Well," he said. "I hope you do."

"Thanks," Sue said brightly, not blinking.

He nodded, the motion jerky, and angled away, choosing a route that took him downhill toward the highway rather than back up toward the house. He stepped carefully, more carefully than a man who knew the ground well would. At the edge of earshot, he raised his hand again, then disappeared behind a ledge, the sound of his footfalls thinning and then gone.

The three women stood very still until the woods settled back around them. A crow complained half-heartedly. Cars rumbled far off. The spirit box went on shredding the air into syllables.

"You don't think he's the one who pushed the boulder that nearly killed us, do you?" Tanya asked, voice low.

Ellen let the question sit just long enough to feel its weight. Bill Kirby's clumsy slide up the hill, his startled wave, his step-watchfulness—none of it read like a man who'd danced across these rocks with lethal confidence.

"Probably not," she said. "Our rock-roller had better footing."

Sue folded her arms, camera balanced in the crook of an elbow. "I don't know," she said slowly. "But I don't like him."

"Neither do I," the spirit box hissed.

They all jumped. Once their hearts stopped trying to leave their bodies, they broke into laughter, the sound ricocheting off stone.

"Okay, Louisa," Sue said, hand to her chest. "You and me both."

Ellen swallowed her grin and reset. "Louisa," she said, pitching her voice toward the rock and the cave and the place all voices go. "Was that man dangerous?"

Static combed the air. Then: "Maybe."

"Was he looking in the right place?" Tanya asked, emboldened.

The box stuttered, then offered a single crisp syllable that could only be what it sounded like: "No."

"Is the treasure here?" Sue asked, unable to keep the eagerness out of her tone.

"There," the box said. Or maybe *near*. The sweep chewed the consonants on its way past. Ellen glanced at the SLS—nothing—then at the EMF—spiking red.

She showed it to her friends.

"Will Sawyer hurt us if we keep looking?" Ellen asked.

Silence. Then a word that fell squarely like a coin in a dish: "Yes."

A cold pinched the bridge of Ellen's nose the way headaches announce themselves. She breathed through it. Tanya shivered visibly. Sue's mouth flattened.

"We want peace," Sue said gently, the way you talk to a skittish horse. "We want you at peace, too. Can you help us to convince Sawyer that Alf isn't coming back for that treasure?"

The box cackled and then spit a sound that might have been a laugh. In Ellen's pocket, the EMF flashed to yellow—two bars—then dropped. On the ridge above them, a jay let loose with an indignant screech.

"Last questions," Ellen said, aware of the light slipping down the trunks like someone pouring pale molasses. "Louisa, can we help you? Do you want us to do anything for you?"

The answer came slower this time, grained with the sweep's insistence. "Help . . . him."

"Help who?" Tanya asked, leaning in. "Alf?"

"No," the box said.

"Sawyer?" Ellen asked.

The spirit box was silent for at least ten seconds before it spat, "Yes."

They went very still. The word hung there, ordinary and extraordinary at once.

"We can do that," Sue said, voice unexpectedly thick. "How can we help him? What does he need?"

They waited for a full minute, but the box made no intelligible reply.

Ellen thought of the humming in the condo, the way the space had pulled a half-tune out of her without permission. She didn't sing now—not yet—but she filed it the way she filed measurements and routes and where she'd set her keys.

"All right," Ellen finally said. "We're going to go for today. Thank you for talking with us, Louisa." She reached out and stroked the red ribbon. "We're leaving this here for you. It's our promise that we'll be back."

She powered down the spirit box. The sudden absence of its buzz felt like stepping into a quieter room. The birds filled the gap. The hollow breathed.

They packed with practiced economy, coiling cords, capping lenses, checking for stray batteries the way mothers check for stray mittens. As she zipped the pouch, Ellen looked down in the direction Bill Kirby had gone and, unbidden, pictured him again—bald head flashing between trees, that slight hitch in his stride, the pale flare of his face when Sue had tossed her pebble.

"Think he'll be back?" Tanya asked, following her gaze.

"Oh, definitely," Sue said, shouldering her bag. "They always come back."

"We better be ready for him," Ellen said, less as a threat than as a promise to herself.

They climbed the hill slowly, the bags heavier on the way up, the gravity of the day tugging a little at their knees. At the top, the Victorian waited—new paint drying, men talking, old memories clinging.

On the porch, Caleb stepped out, wiping his hands. "Still good," he said, before they could ask. "Drawers behaving."

"Excellent," Sue said, bright, like a woman keeping two plates spinning and refusing to let either wobble.

Inside, the parlor's moody blue walls looked calmer than they had that morning, as if the house had resigned itself to kindness despite itself. Ellen paused in the entry to listen again—men working, floorboards settling, the faint cough of the compressor. The living world in all its ordinary racket.

"You think Ms. Loring's email is waiting for us in your inbox?" Tanya asked Ellen, bringing her from her reverie.

"I hope so," she replied as she pulled her phone from her purse. After opening her email, she sighed. "Not yet."

"Why don't we grab some dinner on the way home?" Sue suggested. "Give her more time to get those letters scanned."

"I'm hungry for pizza and Dr. Pepper," Tanya announced. "Anyone up for takeout and a pizza party in the condo?"

"No pillow fights this time, and you have a deal," Sue teased as she headed for the exit.

They laughed. And for a moment, the thoughts of the man between the trees and the ghost who'd been raped and the boy with the rifle receded, and what they had instead were good friends and the promise of good food and good times.

CHAPTER THIRTEEN

Louisa

The day had bruised into evening—purple sky, neon halos, and the hum of weekend traffic—by the time they left JJ Highway's tight curves behind and eased into Branson's glowing strip. Ellen steered them toward a little pizza place tucked beside a souvenir shop that sold snow globes year-round. Inside, the warmth smelled like garlic and melted cheese; a cooler hummed with rows of sodas. They ordered two large pies—one supreme, one pepperoni—plus an order of Caesar salads because Tanya insisted on at least the *idea* of vegetables, and a six-pack of sodas.

Back at the condo, they kicked off shoes and slid into pajama pants and hoodies, shedding the day's armor. The balcony lights blinked on, reflecting off the slate of Table Rock Lake far in the distance. Ellen set the pizzas on the coffee table and propped her laptop on a stack of coasters. Her phone chimed—an email from Ms. Loring. The subject line read, "Scans: Correspondence Attributed to A. Bolin (Selections)."

"That's Ms. Loring," Ellen cried with a tinge of excitement.

Sue handed out paper plates and napkins. "Showtime!"

Tanya twisted the cap off a soda and took a grateful gulp. "I'm fortified and terrified."

"Perfect mood for reading mail from the 1850s," Ellen said, clicking the email open. A neat list of PDFs waited, each labeled with a date. She downloaded them all, then opened the first.

"June eleven, eighteen fifty-seven," she read, and the condo's soft light seemed to lean closer of its own accord.

She scrolled until black letters found their focus on the screen—Ms. Loring's scans crisp and generous, the paper's faint fiber visible, the ink browned at the edges but legible.

"Ready?" Ellen asked.

Sue and Tanya nodded, pizza slices hovering mid-air like flags at half-mast.

Ellen began.

June 11, 1857

Dear Annabel,

We have crossed so much of Missouri that I dream in fence posts and creeks. Robert Foster's map was good enough to keep us from losing ourselves, and we came to Gamble Farm as he said we should, though we look like we were chewed up by the road and spit out.

Louisa said we must be man and wife to be hired proper, and I said I wish it was true, and she said we would wait until after the conflict. The manager here is named Hadlow. He handed me a guide to their new windmill and said if I could make it work, we could stay.

Robert Foster was right: the farm has been taken over by Unionists to train horses for their cause. But they use the Negroes who are already here for their work just the same, saying it is in service of the greater good. Hypocrites!

The wind fights me, and I fight back. When the wheel finally took and the water came up, Louisa laughed like a twittering bird. The men here are scoundrels, but they are grateful.

Your brother, Alf

Ellen paused, the condo's gentle hum filling in around the words—the fridge cycling on, a faint whir from the balcony HVAC. She swallowed, feeling the pivot in the letter, the world widening for Alf and Louisa.

"Unionists using slave labor," Tanya said grimly. "He's not wrong about the hypocrisy."

"No," Sue agreed.

Ellen scrolled. The next PDF sat below, stamped August 15, 1857. She slid the laptop toward Sue.

"Your turn."

Sue wiped her fingers on a napkin, tugged the computer closer, and read.

August 15, 1857

Dear Annabel,

There is a Negro man here named Harris, and he is like most men I have worked beside in this world, which is to say he wants to finish his work and eat hot food and sleep under a dry roof. He uses his hands like they were educated.

He told me in a whisper that last week Hadlow hung three white men down at the creek for stealing horses and there was no trial to it. They jerked and fouled themselves and their faces went purple before the stillness took them, and Harris said he hopes to never see such a thing again. He would not eat for a day afterwards.

A month from then, after I got the windmill to work without me standing and praying over it, Louisa and I set to take horses in the night. We had our leads ready and our hearts, too. Harris came to us with saddles and bridles. I asked him why he helped us, and he said he was glad for the fresh water from the windmill and wanted to thank me properly.

For the first time in my seventeen years, I think maybe the Negroes have souls, same as us. Even so, I still believe they were given to us by God to be our helpers.

Your brother, Alf

Sue exhaled hard through her nose. "There's a crack."

Tanya set her pizza down. "Harris's grace is doing more for him than Miss Fulton ever did."

Ellen felt a tenderness she didn't want to feel—infuriating and human. "It's one thing to argue ideas," she said. "It's another to be handed a bridle by the person you've been taught to think of as an object."

"Of course," Sue said. "And yet." She mimed a scale with her hands. "On one side, a stirred conscience. On the other, what he does next."

"Next letter?" Tanya asked softly. Ellen nodded and passed her the laptop.

Tanya scrolled to March 23, 1858, and began, her voice smoothing into the cadence of the page.

March 23, 1858

Dear Annabel,

We are in Kansas now where everything is different. We fell in with the Sumner boys—two brothers who can shoot straight—and a man called Ouellette who speaks French and English. Louisa knows some French from her mother's side, mostly nursery rhymes.

We agreed that our work is to slow the Union men and the Free Staters for the sake of the Secessionists.

The Free Staters say each state can decide its own way, which sounds fine to a man on his porch, but the truth of it is a fire that runs if you give it a wind.

We ride up on homesteads, and I ask where a man sits. If he is Free State, we take what we want. If he is Union, we take everything. If he is Secesh, we share coffee and a laugh.

I miss Missouri. Kansas is a table, and the wind blows straight across.

Louisa says hello.

Your brother, Alf

"What a hellish existence for everyone," Sue muttered.

Ellen reached for the laptop, the impulse to keep moving—keep breathing—strong. She opened the file dated September 1, 1858.

September 1, 1858

Dear Annabel,

We found a covered wagon on the road with a family of six in it, and I cannot fathom how they have survived thus far with no guns and no meat, only bread and onions and a little bag for their coins. They said they were Secessionists moving south.

I did not take their bread. I did find a pretty dress that fits Louisa. Louisa laughed until she cried when she put it on, then she took it off and gave it back, saying it wouldn't suit a soldier for the cause.

We followed the family south, the smell of onions from the wagon making us weep.

Your brother, Alf

Tanya snorted. "Onions made them weep—not terrorizing human beings, but the smell of onions."

"At least Louisa didn't take the dress," Sue put in.

Ellen blinked. The next scan in the list—February 5, 1859—caused her fingers to hesitate on the trackpad in a new way. Alf wouldn't know it, but at age seventeen, he had only four remaining years on this earth. She opened it.

She had to take a breath before she began. The condo seemed to shift, the walls leaning in as if to brace them.

February 5, 1859

Dear Annabel,

I've been carrying this letter in my coat for weeks, not knowing if I had the right to write it at all.

Louisa's gone.

We went after that trading post I wrote you of. When we got there, smoke already blackened the sky. Another gang—Secesh, from the looks of their flag—had come first. The Sumner brothers rushed in, wild for plunder. I told Louisa to hold the horses, but gunfire cracked like thunder, and the world went mad.

By the time I found my way back, she was gone. The others said they saw riders dragging her into the trees. I spent two days tracking her through ash, mud, and blood till I found her on the riverbank, barely breathing. She couldn't stand, couldn't even look at me. Her clothes were ripped, and she had cuts and bruises all over. Her beautiful, red hair had been burned to the scalp. She just whispered one word: "Secesh" before she went unconscious.

I took her to the Fosters, the closest place I knew, but she died two days later. I buried her not far from there beneath the sycamores and swore on her grave that I'd make those devils pay for what they did.

Your brother, Alf

Ellen didn't realize she'd been gripping the couch cushion until her fingers ached. The room felt both very small and very large—a tunnel and a sky.

Tanya stared at the dark window where their reflections hovered ghostlike over the city lights, her soda forgotten on the table. Sue wiped her cheek with the back of her hand and shook her head once, hard, as if to dislodge an image.

No one spoke for a moment. The only sounds were the slick slide of a car on the street below and the soft thrum of the fridge. Ellen felt the old animal bristle—the instinct to lift her lip at the world and show teeth. But braided through it was something else she hated to recognize: understanding. Not forgiveness—not even close—but the shape of the engine that had driven a boy into a man who had chosen wrong over and over in the name of something he told himself was right.

"He blamed the people he already hated," Tanya said finally, voice hushed. "Even when it was his own."

"And then he made everybody pay," Sue said. "Union, Free State, Secesh—didn't matter, as long as someone bled."

Ellen rubbed her thumb over the laptop's cool edge. "And somewhere in there is Sawyer, taking notes on how to guard a thing with a gun."

They sat with it. The pizza congealed on the plates, grease turning opaque. The sodas went flat.

"I think that's enough for tonight," Sue said gently. "We can't carry more of this and sleep."

"Agreed," Tanya said, already gathering plates like she could tidy grief into the trash.

Ellen closed the laptop, the click oddly final. She slid it into the sleeve, then leaned forward, elbows on knees, and pressed her fingertips to her closed eyes. When she lowered her hands, her vision felt rinsed.

"I'm going to call Brian," she said, and tried to make it sound casual.

"Tell him we ate our vegetables," Tanya said.

"And that we miss him," Sue added.

Ellen smiled at both of them and slipped into the small bedroom she shared with Sue. The twin beds looked like boats. From her nightstand, she picked up her phone and thumbed Brian's contact. He answered on the second ring, his voice a balm as familiar as the dent in their couch at home.

"Hey, you," he said. "How's Branson?"

"Cold. Haunted. Overachieving," she said, and he laughed the way she'd hoped he would.

They traded small things—how Moseby had tried to bury a slipper in the laundry basket; how the neighbor's oak had dropped a limb but missed the fence; how Brian had attempted a new chili recipe and might have invented a biohazard.

"Did you have a good day?" he asked at last, tone reaching for the dip in hers.

"Productive," she said, opting for the truth she could hand him without asking him to hold the rest. "We visited an archive. We read old letters. We ate pizza. We learned more than we wanted to."

"That last one seems to be a theme when you travel with Sue and Tanya."

"Accurate," she said, smiling. "How's my Moseby?"

Brian's voice seemed far away when he said, "Say hi to Mom, Moseby."

A thin, indignant bark scratched warm against her ear.

"Hi, sweet boy," Ellen cooed, eyes stinging again for reasons that had nothing to do with onions. "Be good for Dad."

"He misses you," Brian said softly. "I do, too."

"I'll be home soon," she promised. "We've got a lot to do, but I'll be home."

They said their goodnights, the familiar rhythm of it setting a gentler cadence in her bones. When the call ended, the room seemed kinder. Sue had already slipped in, pulled on an eye mask, and burrowed under the quilt.

Ellen crossed to her bed and slid beneath the covers. The sheets were cool; the pillow cupped her head. She turned toward the window, where the city's glitz made soft patterns on the blinds. She thought of Louisa's last word—*Secesh*—and of the men who had used allegiance as an excuse to unmake a person.

She closed her eyes and offered a brief prayer. Let the house hold. Let the men keep working. Let the woods keep their rocks on the hillside. Let the ghosts tell the truth or leave the living be. Let the women—she and Sue and Tanya—stay brave and whole and smart enough to walk away when the cliff gave way underfoot.

Sleep came in small waves. When she finally drifted, she dreamed of a riverboat's whistle bending itself into a lullaby, and of a red ribbon tied to a low branch moving in wind that was only half wind, half breath.

CHAPTER FOURTEEN

The Titanic

By late Saturday morning the Strip was already awake—billboards blinking, tour buses idling, the bright carnival of Branson humming to itself like a radio just off-station. Ellen steered them down the hill and into town, the Chevy Onix a little sticky from yesterday's leaf dust, all three of them quieter than usual. Sleep had come—but not the kind that erases ugly images.

"Carb therapy," Sue declared from the back seat as she spotted the red tin roof and white farmhouse facade. "Doctor's orders."

"Whose doctor?" Tanya asked from the front passenger's seat.

"Mine," Sue said, patting her chest. "Dr. Pancake."

The Farmhouse Restaurant smelled exactly like its name: butter and coffee and bacon. A hostess with a snowflake pin on her apron led them to a corner booth where a window framed a square of winter sky and the street's steady motion. The room had that cozy clatter Ellen loved—plates gliding, silverware chiming, the low bass of conversation.

They ordered without pretending to be virtuous: blueberry pancakes and sausage for all; a side of hash browns "for the table," which meant everyone would pretend not to want them and then eat them. Hot tea for Ellen and Tanya, coffee for Sue.

"To our health," Sue said when the mugs arrived, lifting hers like it contained courage. "Can you tell that I've lost two more pounds? Though, I'm about to gain them back again with this breakfast."

"You look great," Tanya said. "You and Ellen both are putting me to shame on this trip with your fancy clothes. I really need to level up."

"Like we said," Ellen began, running her fingers along the V-neck of her navy cashmere sweater, "you look great in anything."

"What's on tap for today?" Sue asked before sipping her coffee.

"We said we'd go to the Titanic Museum, remember?" Tanya dapped a napkin to the corner of her mouth.

"That's right," Ellen said. "Titanic first. We'll let the dead talk after we've had pancakes and a history field trip."

The pancakes arrived in rounds the size of 78 RPM records, studded with berries that bled purple into the golden cake. Syrup came in warm little pitchers that steamed when you tipped them. Sausage links lay beside them, like punctuation marks.

By the second bite, color had returned to Tanya's cheeks. "I can feel my soul reattaching," she said. "And yes, I know the theological problems with that sentence."

From the Farmhouse, it was a short drive—two traffic lights, a turn—before the Titanic Museum rose into view, its façade a dramatic, almost surreal prow cleaving the low winter light. The full-scale partial replica did something to Ellen's stomach: a tug, a tilt, a whisper of vertigo. The iceberg "mountain" hunched alongside, pale and theatrical. A lamppost out front bore a brass plaque. Families posed for photos beneath the lifelike rivets.

"Okay, this is cool," Sue admitted, even as she made a face like she should be above such tourist bait. "Giant ship in a parking lot? I'm in."

"Best kind of cognitive dissonance," Tanya said.

Inside, the temperature seemed to drop half a degree, whether by design or imagination. A young docent in period servant's clothing—black dress, white apron—stood at a lectern with a stack of tickets. Her hair was neat beneath a little cap. She smiled with the professional brightness of someone who had said the same thirty sentences all week and still liked them.

"Welcome aboard," she said, handing Ellen a stiff card the size of a postcard. "You are now a passenger on the RMS Titanic. Explore the ship at your leisure. By the end of your journey, you may discover your fate."

Ellen glanced down. The card read: *Caroline Lane Brown, Age 59, First Class.*

"That sounds . . . fancy," Ellen said.

Sue flipped her card. "Charlotte Lamson Appleton, First Class. Ooh, I feel rich."

Tanya read hers aloud. "Malvina Helen Cornell, First Class. What if I get bossy?"

"You already are," Sue said sweetly, and dodged a halfhearted elbow. "Oh, wait. I'm the bossy one."

The three friends and the young docent laughed.

"Be sure to explore for clues to your fate aboard the Titanic," the young docent reminded them with a grin.

Beyond the lectern, another attendant offered small handheld devices and headphones for the self-guided audio tour. They each clipped one to a lanyard and slipped on their headsets. A man's voice, warm and British, bloomed in Ellen's ears, welcoming them aboard, setting the scene. Couples milled around them, mouthing *wow* at the grand staircase replica ahead—oak-paneled, sweeping, the cherub lamp at its base.

Ellen's audio guide launched into the Titanic's specs—the pride of Belfast, nearly 900 feet long; the "unsinkable" marvel. She'd heard the facts before, yet the list always took her breath away—so much skill and hubris and hope woven into a single object. They moved with the trickle of the crowd, taking in glass cases that held artifacts—porcelain teacups with the White Star Line flag; a letter to a mother; a pocket watch stopped at 2:28. A steward's jacket hung behind glass, the cuffs softly frayed where a man's hands had worried them in habit or cold.

"Look," Tanya said, tugging Ellen's sleeve toward a framed photo and a paragraph caption. "Charlotte Appleton."

Sue leaned in to read. Her audio guide beeped as it found the proper track. "Charlotte Lamson Appleton accompanied by her sisters Malvina Cornell and Caroline Lane Brown—oh!" She turned to her friends, eyes wide. "We were sisters!"

Tanya and Ellen looked down at their cards and then back up at the photo. In the black-and-white, three women in fashionable clothes looked sternly and solemnly at the camera. The caption explained that the sisters were travelling home to New York from Britain, where they had attended the funeral of their sister, Lady Drummond.

"What are the odds?" Ellen asked, delighted and spooked.

"Statistically, with curated options, higher than random," Tanya said—then shivered. "But still."

They drifted together through the "First Class" rooms, marveling at the recreated suite—the rich damask, the private sitting room. Past that, the mock hallway narrowed to "Third Class"—rows of tiny bunks; tin cups on a shelf; a sign about stew. Ellen trailed her hand along the smooth railing. An exhibit labeled "Iceberg Wall" invited visitors to press their palms to a slab of freezing surface set to twenty-eight degrees—the temperature of the North Atlantic that night. Sue dared first, yelping, then insisted both friends try.

"That's not nice," Tanya said, jerking her hand back. "My bones felt that."

"Imagine minutes in that," Ellen said softly. "Or worse."

In a little side gallery, a violin lay in a glass case—a replica, the placard specified, but the plaque told the story of Wallace Hartley, the bandmaster who kept playing to steady panic. The audio narrator's voice gentled for the tale, the string quartet's music barely audible beneath it, like a remembered lullaby.

"You're crying," Sue said, nudging Ellen with her shoulder.

"I'm not crying," Ellen said, touching the corner of her eye. "It's just cold in here."

They stepped onto the "boat deck," where the museum had rigged a tilted floor at different gradients so visitors could test their footing at five, ten, fifteen degrees. Sue planted herself at ten and spread her arms, grinning. "I am Rose," she declared. "With better lashes."

"Get down before you pull something," Tanya said, though she smiled despite herself.

Ellen's awareness of time grew watery. The museum was good at building a narrative—rooms widening and narrowing, artifacts pressed close, then small balconies of air to look down into the central staircase. Still, her chest had a pressure in it that wasn't entirely the structure, and the hair rose on the back of her neck more than once, as if she was reliving the past. She reached to steady herself and felt Sue's hand already there.

"You okay?" Sue whispered.

"Yeah," Ellen said. "Just woozy. Like I know this place."

"Past life woozy?" Tanya asked, half-joking.

Ellen opened her mouth to brush it away. Then she didn't. The three names on their cards sat in her brain like pebbles in a row.

Another gallery displayed personal effects recovered from the wreck: a tiny perfume vial that still held the ghost of scent; a woman's beaded bag, shabby now, but once carefully chosen. In this room, a little—almost negligible—scent of salt seemed to thread the air. Intellect told Ellen it was theater. Something older told her to breathe shallowly.

They paused beside a panel with a sepia photograph of three women on a New York City street—not Titanic women, just women of the era. Still, all three braced in a similar way—relief and shock and purpose. Sue tapped the glass, then snatched her hand back as if the image might disapprove.

"Listen," Ellen said, nodding at her audio guide. The narrator was telling the story of lifeboat 6—of a woman pleading to turn back, of others refusing, of the night's cruel math. A piece floated into place uninvited: a feeling of wood beneath her gloves, sea breath burning her nose, the terrible bliss of a lantern appearing where there had been dark.

"Okay," Tanya said after a beat, voice paper-thin. "I'm—this is—weird."

"Yup," Sue said softly. "It's like my bones have a story I forgot to read."

They found a case labeled "Appleton/Cornell." Sue bent close. Charlotte and her sister, Malvina, went up on deck and survived the sinking by boarding Lifeboat Two, which left the ship very late, at 1:40 A.M.; her other sister, Caroline Lane Brown, had become separated from her sisters. With the help of Colonel Archibald Gracie, she boarded and survived upon Collapsible D, which was the last lifeboat to be lowered by the davits.

"I was afraid I'd never see you two again," Ellen murmured absently.

"What did you say?" Sue demanded, eyes wide.

Tanya sighed. "I remember." She covered her mouth. "I need to sit down."

"I need to use the restroom," Ellen said, suddenly feeling faint.

"We'll wait for you in the lobby," Sue promised.

The ladies' room was hushed, the air warm and fragranced with a generic floral scent. Ellen slipped into a stall, grateful for the banal privacy. In Hot Springs, when she and her friends had learned they'd been soul mates with common past lives, Ellen had been mesmerized, finally able to draw clear lines between dreams and memories. She and her friends had visited other mediums, investigating who they'd been, and never once had anything about the Titanic surfaced. Ellen had had plenty of dreams about sinking ships, but it had never dawned on her, not in her wildest nightmares, that they were hints of a past she'd shared with her friends. They'd been on the Titanic, and they'd survived.

When she emerged and reached the sinks, the mirror reflected her state of mind—hair a little flyaway from the headset, cheeks pink from cold exhibits and warm tears. She reached for the faucet and froze.

Another woman stood behind her in the mirror. Ellen hadn't heard her approach.

Her dress was black with a high white collar, hair pinned in a severe knot at the back of her head. She must be a museum attendant, Ellen thought, though her face was pale in the mirror's light, eyes dark, the mouth composed in a way that seemed otherworldly.

Ellen's breath hitched. She turned, a small, automatic smile lifting. "Oh, I—excuse me."

No one stood there.

She stared at empty air. The soap dispenser chirped as if to break the spell; a toilet flushed behind a closed stall. Ellen turned back to the mirror.

The woman remained there, behind her reflection, as if the glass had kept what the room had let go. The woman lifted her chin a fraction.

"Help him," she said. The voice bloomed against the inside of Ellen's skull—too close, as if spoken with a hand cupped around the words.

Ellen's mouth went dry. "Help who?" she whispered, lips trembling in a way that made her feel ridiculous and terribly young.

The woman didn't answer. She was simply gone. Not a fade— one frame, then nothing.

Ellen grabbed the faucet, turned the hot water on full, and leaned into the steam. The roar steadied her, the warmth opening her lungs. She washed her hands mechanically, then stood there, watching the mirror cloud. Her reflection went soft, then disappeared under a layer of white.

Slowly, as if drawn by a child's fingertip, letters appeared through the condensation—tracks where the steam refused to cling: S-A-W-Y-E-R.

The name wrote itself into being. Ellen's scalp prickled. For a second she pictured a teenage boy's hand scrawling through breath, a secret message to a girl he'd made into a confessor.

"Louisa?" Ellen called. No, that hadn't been Louisa. The woman in the mirror had been too old. And her hair had not been red.

"Okay," Ellen said aloud, to the sink, to herself, to the air. Her voice sounded wrong in the tiled room—too clear. At first, she thought of getting her friends to come look, to see if they saw it, too. But when another woman emerged from a stall and turned toward the sinks, Ellen pressed a paper towel to the mirror, blotting the word. It smeared but did not quite disappear.

When she pushed back into the hallway, her heartbeat felt like it had moved into her throat. She spotted Sue and Tanya in the next gallery, standing beneath the wall where names were engraved and a brass rail ran at waist height. The room murmured with families softly reading out names and fates—survived, lost—like a litany.

Tanya saw Ellen's face before Ellen reached them and put both hands up like she could catch whatever was spilling. "What happened?"

Ellen told them—her voice flat at first, then gathering speed like a car on an open slope. She left nothing out, not even the quiver in her lips, the way her body had wanted to run and stay simultaneously.

"Help *him*," Sue repeated, eyes wide. "And then *Sawyer*."

Ellen nodded. "In the mirror. Like someone wrote it with a finger. I tried to blot it, and it didn't want to go."

"I vote we don't stand in front of any more mirrors today," Tanya said, trying for levity and landing somewhere between joke and plea. "Also, I would like a snack."

"We'll get you a snack," Sue said, voice gentle. She turned to the wall and ran a finger over the etched Charlotte L. Appleton and Malvina H. Cornell, then to Caroline L. Brown. "All three survived," she said softly. "At least there's that."

"And now they want us to help a boy who kills people," Tanya said, grim again.

Ellen leaned against the rail and let the cool brass anchor her. Beneath her palm, thousands of hands had hovered here, touched, then withdrawn. In her pocket, her phone buzzed—the phantom memory of Ms. Loring's email earlier, scans waiting. She swallowed.

"Let's go home," she said. "Finish the letters. Watch last night's footage. If Sawyer's asking for help . . ." she trailed off, the word *help* jangling against *murderer* in her head like mismatched bells. "If he's asking, there's something we need to see."

"Or he's luring us," Sue said with narrowed eyes.

"Or both," Ellen said. "We'll be careful."

They returned their audio devices and stepped back into the lobby, where the gift shop glittered with the ship in miniature, tea towels printed with deck plans, children's captain hats, and peppermints in tins stamped with old fonts. The docent at the lectern smiled as they passed, oblivious to the shift in oxygen they carried with them.

Outside, the cold bit their cheeks. The parking lot felt simultaneously absurd and grounding—minivans, sun glare on windshields, a toddler throwing a shoe while his mother negotiated surrender.

"Who do you think the woman was?" Tanya asked as they walked. "Caroline? Charlotte? Malvina? Someone else?"

"Wrong dress for first class," Ellen said before she could stop herself. She didn't know how she knew, except that the cut had said *work*, not *leisure*. "A steward? Someone who helped people into boats?"

"Or a sister," Sue said softly. "Not one of us—the other kind. The habit kind."

Ellen considered it and felt the click of plausibility. "A nun," she said. "I think you're right."

Back at the condo, after beers and burgers at the Buzzard Bar, the afternoon light had thinned. They brewed tea, the mundane ritual widening the gap between their museum visit and now. Ellen opened her laptop to Ms. Loring's email again and scrolled the list—more dates, more ink across years.

"Ready?" she asked, even as the word felt too small for whatever they were opening.

"Ready," Sue said, sliding a coaster under her mug like a woman who refused to let water rings mark a rented table.

"Ready," Tanya echoed, hugging a throw pillow to her stomach like armor.

They took their places—Ellen in the middle with the laptop with Sue on one side, Tanya on the other. Outside, the Strip's neon had not yet bloomed; the sky held to its pale blue a little longer like a boy refusing to let go of a tree branch across a creek.

Ellen opened the next scan and took a breath, feeling the museum ghost and the mirror word and the boy in the woods gather on the couch with them. Whatever story Sawyer wanted told, whatever help a dead child could request, would have to thread through Alf's letters. The past had laid out a path; the present had pointed at it in steam.

"Okay," she said. "Let's see what they have to say."

CHAPTER FIFTEEN

Sawyer

Sue cupped her mug of tea and nodded toward the laptop. "Let's finish it tonight. No more dragging ghosts into Sunday."

"Agreed," Tanya said. "And maybe afterward we can watch something mind-numbing. Like a baking show."

Ellen smiled faintly, though her stomach felt heavy. "Okay. July ninth, eighteen fifty-nine." She scrolled until the sepia-toned scan filled the screen.

July 9, 1859

Dear Annabel,

Two days after I buried Louisa, I found a boy not far off, curled up behind a log and crying into his knees. He'd seen what was done to her. Said his name was Sawyer, and he'd been following me. Twelve years old, come down on an orphan train from New York. Some farmer west of here picked him and worked him near to death, and when he ran off, they called him thief and halfwit. He said he just wanted a family that didn't hit.

He told me he'd joined with some men for food and that those same men were the ones who hurt Louisa. He didn't know what they planned until it started. Then he ran. I could see it in his eyes—he'll never outrun it. Neither will I.

So, I took him with me. Then he said he wanted to help me find the ones who did it. He knows where they hang out. Pray we find them, for Louisa.

Your brother, Alf

Ellen exhaled slowly. The hum of the refrigerator filled the silence that followed.

"Poor kid," Tanya said. "Imagine witnessing that at twelve."

"Imagine living with Alf afterward," Sue murmured. "Revenge is a bad apprenticeship."

Ellen scrolled, her finger trembling slightly. "Next one's March twenty-first, eighteen sixty. Sue?"

Sue took the laptop, pulling her glasses down from her head.

March 21, 1860

Dear Annabel,

The deed is done, and I write this with hands that still shake. Sawyer found them—six men camped at Bush Creek. He knew the place; they'd first taken him there when they made him swear their oaths. They'd called him Shrimp, the bastards. He said nothing, just led me there like a bloodhound on the scent for God's own reckoning.

We waited until dawn. I told him to stay back, but when the first man stepped out to piss, Sawyer was already sighting down the rifle. He never missed. By the time the sun was up, all six lay still. I spared only the dog. She was a hound bitch, trembling so hard her teeth clicked. I wanted to put her out of her misery, but Sawyer started crying again. We named her Louisa instead.

He's a simple boy but pure-hearted. He looks to me like a father, and I find myself answering like one. Maybe that's what the Almighty planned when He left me breathing. Don't worry, Annabel. No one will ever take your place, but it is good to have someone who is devoted to me.

Your brother, Alf

Sue looked up from the screen. "He's grooming him," she said flatly. "Turning that poor kid into his mirror."

"Or into his weapon," Tanya added.

Ellen stared at her tea. "And Louisa's name lives on as a dog."

"Poetic in a twisted way," Sue said. She pushed the laptop toward Tanya. "Next up, September nineteenth, eighteen sixty."

September 19, 1860

Dear Annabel,

After leaving you in Springfield, I felt a peace I didn't deserve, but it didn't last. Sawyer and I stopped at a store to buy tobacco and fell in with a pair of roughs talking big about homestead raids. Before I knew it, I was buying them drinks and telling tales. They were ours before the bottle ran dry. By week's end we'd gathered six more—including the Sumner boys again and old Ouellette—and we were twelve, not counting the dog.

I led them south to Taney County where the caves cut clean through the hills. From there we can see the road running north and south, wagons crawling like ants. It's a fine place for a man to disappear—or to make others disappear. We'll keep Missouri safe from foreigners who think to own her soul. Sawyer keeps the watch. The boy's eyes never sleep.

Your brother, Alf

Sue whispered, "Murder Rocks."

Ellen's stomach gave a small twist. "And Sawyer is there."

Tanya nodded. "The caves, the road—that's exactly where we were standing the other day."

Ellen took the laptop again, scrolling until the next letter opened.

April 2, 1861

Dear Annabel,

We've been busy, my Merry Men and me. We've struck three wagon trains this month, all carrying gold or silver for the Union cause. We wear their coats, wave their flags, and take what we can. We only kill when there's no other choice. Sawyer is a good shot.

The dog alerts before any stranger comes near. Sometimes I swear she hears the clink of coin in a pocket. I keep the loot buried deep in the cave under the largest rock—you'd laugh if you saw it, sister, looks like it's been dropped from the sky. Maybe one day, when all this foolishness is ended, you'll visit and I'll show you what a man can build out of vengeance and luck.

Your brother, Alf

"'Under the largest rock,'" Sue repeated, eyebrows up. "That sounds like an engraved invitation."

"Probably long gone," Tanya said. "But still."

"Still." Ellen scrolled. The next file bore the date of June 30, 1861.

June 30, 1861

Dear Annabel,

The war has come and Missouri wears the wrong colors. Union blue! It burns me to think our people would turn against their own. So, I punish them the only way I can—by taking their gold, their silver, their pride. The cave is near full now. Sawyer says we should move it before someone stumbles on it, but I think not. No one will look where death whispers.

Some of the men talk of heading east to fight with the army. Fools. They'll die for generals who never knew their names. Here we make our own rules, our own country. When this is done, I'll come to you with what's left and we'll live a rich, quiet life.

Think of me, Annabel. I'll be thinking of you.

Your brother, Alf

Ellen's throat tightened. "And this is it," she said quietly. "The last one before he dies."

Sue nodded, scrolling to the final PDF. The page looked more fragile than the rest, the ink feathered like breath on cold glass.

December 12, 1862

Dear Annabel,

Some of the boys grumbled today. Said they wanted their split and to go home for Christmas. A couple even talked of joining the Confederate Army—said we'd done our part and they wanted proper uniforms, proper cause. I told them this is the cause. Guerilla war is the only true fight left. I gave them a speech that near lifted the roof from the cave, about freedom and vengeance and gold, and all but two came back to sense.

Before I could fetch the other two down from the ridge, Sawyer got to them. Didn't even know he was up there in the tree—quiet as a fox. One shot each. Dropped them like bad thoughts. He came down calm as Sunday and said, "They were gonna quit." I told him he shouldn't have done it, but inside I knew it was a lesson worth learning for the rest. The men won't question me again.

Happy Christmas, Sister. Don't forget to think of me. I will be thinking of you.

Your brother, Alf

Sue looked up from the screen. "And that's the last one."

Ellen rubbed her temples. "So, Sawyer murdered two men to keep Alf's gang in line. A twelve-year-old turned executioner."

"Sawyer would have been fourteen by then," Sue pointed out.

"Still." Tanya hugged the throw pillow harder.

They sat in silence for a moment. Outside, traffic whispered on the highway like a distant river. The condo's heater clicked on, blowing warm air across their cheeks.

Tanya took another sip of her tea. "So where do we go from here?"

Ellen closed her laptop, seeing the ghost of the words anyway. "Back to Murder Rocks," she said finally. "We need to talk to Sawyer."

Tanya gave a nervous laugh. "Because he sounds so approachable?"

"Because he's the key," Ellen said.

"Whatever we do," Tanya began with a sigh, "let's not forget that that ghost managed to kill Jason Albright and push a boulder that nearly took us down, too. He's powerful, ladies, and not to be underestimated."

They sat a while longer, the hum of the heater filling the space between thought and speech. The letters lay heavy on their hearts—the boy who wanted a family, the man who taught him vengeance, and the centuries-old echo of violence still clinging to the hills outside Branson.

CHAPTER SIXTEEN

A Vengeful Spirit

Ellen woke to the soft hiss of rain against the condo's balcony glass and the bitter comfort of strong coffee cooling in her hands. Sue had commandeered the dining table with hard drives, labeled SD cards, and a scatter of Post-its that fluttered whenever the heater kicked on. Tanya—in plaid pajama pants and an oversized college hoodie—sat cross-legged on the sofa, hugging a throw pillow the way some people held rosary beads.

"Okay," Sue said, tapping a pen against their notebook. "Murder Rocks review. We start with my full-spectrum footage from two nights ago, then the static cam, then the EVPs. And before either of you asks—yes, I triple-backed up the audio."

Ellen tried to smile as she touched the marks on the back of her neck. "I wasn't going to ask," she said, which earned her a grin from Tanya.

"Liar," Tanya murmured.

They sat around the kitchen table with mugs of coffee, toasted bagels, Sue's laptop, and their recording devices.

On Sue's screen, her full-spectrum footage jittered into life: the narrow beam of a headlamp cutting through cedar and oak, a lattice of limestone outcrops that locals had named Murder Rocks a century and a half ago. It always looked more ordinary in daylight, but at night it became angles and shadows, a chessboard where the next move could crush you.

Sue clicked. The angle switched to the static camera they'd wedged between two stones, aimed at the wide slash of path where the boulder had rolled. Ellen's throat cinched when she saw it happen again: the sudden pivot, the loosened stone that should've stayed put and didn't, the boulder shouldering itself free and barrel-rolling through the weeds as if shoved by a pair of invisible hands. On screen, Ellen's gasp from two days ago came back to her: raw, startled, and sharp. She watched their bodies scramble. Watched herself freeze for that one heartbeat, the old teacher instinct in her saying, *Wait—wait—let's think about this*, while the rock chose not to think at all.

Tanya paused the frame where the boulder stopped in a perfect wedge just before the edge of the path. "Do you guys see anything?"

"Nothing," Sue said flatly.

"Let's do the EVPs," Ellen suggested. "The session with Louisa."

Tanya queued the files. Ellen held her breath and listened.

They'd asked the same way they always asked—politely, matter-of-factly, as if they were at a front desk and the clerk had stepped away.

Over the recording, through the static of the spirit box, they heard, *"This is Louisa."*

Then came Ellen's warning, *"It could be a trickster."*

Tanya's voice came next. *"Let's verify."*

"How old were you when you died?" Ellen asked over the recording.

The box hissed, but just before the intelligible answer, "Twenty-two," Ellen heard something else.

Tanya paused the recording. "What was that?"

"It sounded like a growl," Sue replied.

"Play it again," Ellen suggested.

Tanya backed up on the Audacity application to the unexpected spike before hitting play. The sound that came through was low, guttural, and threatening.

Ellen shuddered as she reached back to the scratches on her neck. "That wasn't Louisa."

Over the recording, Sue's voice came next, *"How did you die?"*

Just before the reply that sounded like *Secesh*, there was another guttural sound.

"There!" Ellen cried.

Tanya nodded, having heard it, too. She lined up the curser with the sound wave on Audacity and pressed play. Then she slowed the playback time and played it again. In a deep, low, growl came the words, "Stop talking to them."

Tanya let the recording continue as the three friends listened with wide eyes to the slow playback.

Sue's voice was also slow and lower on the recording: *"We're so sorry, Louisa. We read about you."*

Ellen's reply, also slow and low, *"We need your help."*

But then came another growl, along with the words, *"Ignore them, Louisa."*

Tanya paused the recording. "Do you think that's Sawyer or Alf trying to keep Louisa from talking to us?"

"I think so," Sue replied with a nod. "Let's keep going."

Tanya hit play, and the recording resumed in slow time.

"I've got something," Ellen whispered over the recording. *"Small. Edge of the shelf."*

Then, *"Do you know who killed Jason Albright?"*

The box hissed, then a dark, ominous tone warned, *"I'll kill them,"* before the spirit box spit, *"Yes."*

Tanya paused the recording. "This is terrifying guys. There's something in those woods that wants to kill us."

"Keep going," Ellen prompted.

With a shaky finger, Tanya pressed play.

"Please tell us his or her name," Sue said over the recording.

It was followed by a low, gravelly string of words: *"Don't tell them my name."*

Despite that chilling command, the spirit box replied, *"Sawyer."*

Ellen shivered as the recording played another gravelly string of syllables she couldn't make out. She could hear her own voice recorded over them asking, *"Did it say Sawyer?"* followed by Tanya confirming, *"Yes, Sawyer. Was he protecting Alf's treasure?"*

Beneath their recorded conversation, the ominous growling intensified, and the spirit box began to cackle and hiss. Ellen swore she heard, "I hear footfalls." She glanced at her friends.

"Did you hear that?" she asked them. "I heard 'I hear footfalls.'"

"That was just before Bill Kirby appeared," Sue pointed out.

The recording, still playing, produced stuttering, unintelligible sounds before moving on to their conversation with Bill Kirby.

"Did you hear that?" Tanya cried, stopping the recording. "I thought I heard, 'He's a jerk,' and 'I'll kill him.'"

Tanya played it back.

"Oh, my gawd." Sue sank back in her chair. "This ghost boy has it in for everyone."

Tanya covered her mouth. "Maybe buying this house wasn't a good idea after all. Maybe you should unload it as soon as possible."

"We can't leave it," Sue said. "We can't sell it knowing this is there. We have to deal with him."

"I know," Tanya relented. "You're right."

"If Sawyer thinks he has to stand guard over the treasure for eternity," Ellen said slowly, assembling the thought as it came, "then he needs permission to let it go. He needs somebody he trusts to tell him he can stop. If Louisa's trying to reach him, maybe she needs someone to help her."

"And you think that's us," Tanya said, not asking.

Ellen gave Tanya a look, and Tanya nodded. She already knew the answer, she just didn't like it.

"Of course, it's us," Tanya groaned.

Sue closed the laptop with more force than necessary. "We go back," she said. "Today."

"I agree," Ellen said. "We have no choice."

Tanya looked between them, then sighed, surrendering to what they always did: show up with more kindness than fear and hope it was enough. "Fine. Let's go."

The Victorian was a different creature without Caleb and his crew. No hammer strikes puncturing the day, no electricians shouting from the porch. Only the low conversation of rain in the gutters and the steady drip from a cracked eave into a metal bucket someone had left on the front steps. The house looked almost shy without the bustle.

Sue unlocked the front door. The three of them paused on the threshold as the smell met them: sawdust, old plaster, and damp wood.

"This place is already so beautiful," Tanya said with a sigh. "I'd hate for you to lose it."

"I'm not going to lose it," Sue insisted.

They moved through the main hall, over their faint salt line on the floorboards. Ellen felt the house look at her—the sensation of being measured by a building that knew it had been made to outlast the people in it. She put a hand on the newel post, her palm tightening around it with determination.

"No," she agreed. "You aren't going to lose it."

They grabbed the extra batteries and the second recorder from the dining room table—Caleb had taped a bright orange note there: DON'T STEP ON LOOSE JOISTS. Tanya took a photo and texted back a thumbs-up emoji that would have baffled a nineteenth-century ghost but pleased a twenty-first-century foreman.

Ellen's knee twinged as they navigated the downward slope toward Murder Rocks. She begged it to hold up. Her next steroid injections weren't due for another two months.

Rain had threaded the air into lace; the oaks flicked droplets from above. The limestone shone slick and pale, the path darkened by mud. The world smelled like wet stone and leaves crushed underfoot. The three friends tightened their coats against the chilling breeze.

At the lip of the rocks, Ellen set one of the full-spectrum cameras on a tripod beside the path and the spirit box and EMF detector on a flat bit of stone where Louisa's red ribbon had once been. She wondered if the rain or wind had carried it away, or if Louisa somehow had taken it herself. Ellen flipped on the spirit box, its pulsing cadence out of place in the otherwise dark and quiet woods. Then she picked up the SLS camera and glanced at her friends.

"Are we ready?" Sue held the other full-spectrum camera and had already hit record.

Tanya, wearing her headphones and pointing her mic toward the cave entrance, gave them a thumbs up.

"Sawyer?" Ellen called, pitching her voice calm and low. "It's Ellen, Sue, and Tanya. We came back because you told Louisa to stop talking to us, and we heard you. But we can't stop if we're going to help you."

The spirit box stuttered. A male voice cut between static, stretched thin by the sweep. "Go."

"Wouldn't you like to find peace, Sawyer?" Sue cut in. "Aren't you tired of being stuck down here when you could move on to your eternal rest?"

The EMF spiked, a sudden tick-tick-tick. Ellen's shoulders tightened.

Tanya swallowed. "Sawyer, don't be afraid to move on. From what we've seen, everyone can find redemption and peace, if they want to."

The EMF jumped. On the SLS screen, a stick-figure flickered into existence six feet away: short, thin, one arm lifted. Then it glitched and vanished.

"Sawyer," Ellen said, heart knocking. "You've done your job for a long time. Longer than any boy should have to. The treasure is just metal now. The war is over. Alf has moved on to the other side. Louisa is—" She faltered, not sure if Louisa was stuck here, too, or if she had just come to help. "She wants you to join him. Don't you want to be reunited with your friend?"

A branch cracked somewhere up the slope. They all turned. The skin at Ellen's nape prickled; her knee gave a surprising hot pulse of defiance. "Did you hear—"

Tanya lifted a hand for silence. The woods held its breath. Then, from deeper among the rocks: the heavy, deliberate crunch of a boot. Another. Ellen's eyes darted, tracing where the sound should be and landing only on leaves and the negative space between trees.

"Could be a trespasser," Sue whispered, though her face said she didn't believe it.

Bill Kirby, Ellen thought—Bill, with his water-colored smile and snake-like presence.

"Hello?" she called, surprising herself. "Bill? If that's you, this is not the day."

Silence swallowed her words. Then a whisper-yell in the near distance: "Don't talk to them."

The three women startled together.

"Please," Ellen said, to voice and woods both. She stepped up on a rock for a better vantage point, still unsure whether they were dealing with the living or the dead. "Tell us your name. Who are we talking to?"

Her knee gave a little, so she shifted her weight fully on the other. Then, the world tilted. She felt the push as a cold, flat hand between her shoulder blades—no wind, no balance mistake. A *push*. She pitched forward; her hip slammed stone. White bursts of light popped in her vision.

"Ellen!" Tanya bent beside her on the rock, hands flying uselessly over Ellen's coat as if she could catch pain with her fingers and pocket it. Sue swung around, swore, and dumped the camera on the ground to lift Ellen's head in her hands.

"Did you hit your head?" Sue asked, studying Ellen's eyes for signs of concussion.

"No, my hip," Ellen said as Sue released her to check her legs. "Something pushed me."

The EMF meter chattered. The spirit box yelped syllables like coins clattering: "Stop—stop—stop—"

Ellen dragged in one breath, and then another. She lifted one foot and rotated the ankle—bad, but not broken; the hip would bloom purple by evening. Fear rose in her throat like bile. She swallowed it, then, without getting up from the ground, spoke to the air, hoarse but steady. "Sawyer, listen to me."

Another crunch. Tanya looked up the hill while Sue continued to search Ellen—her elbows, hands—for injuries.

Ellen continued to address the air, "I think you believe it's still your job to guard over Alf's stash. I believe this because you told us to stop trying to find it. But you and I both know what really mattered in that life." She took another breath. The rain was a fine mist now, settling in her hair. "It wasn't metal in the ground. It wasn't the men who used you. It was you and Alf watching each other's backs in a world that was torn up and dangerous. It was the two of you being there for each other while the rest of the world burned."

The wind moved—or maybe it didn't. Ellen heard more footfalls in the distance, but she focused on trying to reach Sawyer.

Tanya and Sue stood over her, listening for signs from the beyond.

"You were a boy," Ellen said, and her voice broke on the word. "A boy who had to become a man too soon. Louisa wants you to be a boy again long enough to let go. She wants you to join her and Alf on the other side."

Somewhere above them, a sharp crack split the air. Ellen glanced up and saw the thick, rotting limb of an oak give way. Time stuttered into a slow crawl. The branch rotated, end over end, all that weight choosing a path that ended with her.

"Move!" Sue lunged, grabbing under Ellen's arms; Tanya scrambled at her feet, bracing herself to take Ellen's weight.

Ellen tried to stand. The ankle refused. Pain shot up her leg, and she made a sound she would have been embarrassed to hear if she'd had time to think.

Not fast enough, Ellen thought. *We are not fast enough.*

The branch halted in midair.

It wasn't a pause or a glitch. It was a halt, as complete as a period. Bark dust drifted down on Ellen's cheeks; she tasted the wet green of it on her tongue. Her ears roared. Sue froze in the act of pulling Ellen out of the branch's path. Tanya's mouth opened around a word she didn't finish.

The figure holding the branch stood three paces away, both arms braced above her head, palms flat against wood. She was young and solid, not the gauze of most apparitions but something with edges, each hair of her vibrant red head distinct as if a match had been struck behind it. The trousers rode low on narrow hips, suspenders slung over a linen shirt, sleeves rolled to reveal forearms. Boots planted. Eyes—God, the eyes—like river glass.

"Run," the apparition shouted in a whisper, the sound doubled as if it came both from the mouth and from the space in front of it.

The three women jolted into motion. Sue hauled Ellen upright; Tanya wedged herself under Ellen's other arm. They sidestepped on the stones, Ellen's ankle screaming, hip a drumbeat of pain. The branch sagged a few inches, then steadied again as the girl adjusted her grip. Ellen couldn't take her eyes off the impossible angle of those arms, the determination knitted into that young jaw.

"Louisa," Tanya breathed.

The apparition's gaze flicked to them, and something like a smile ghosted across her mouth—wry and sad, as if she'd seen every foolish thing humans did for love and forgiven all of them.

Sue, still holding Ellen, lifted her chin. "If we're going to help Sawyer," she said, "we need you, Louisa. Help us convince him it's not his job to protect the treasure. Tell him he can move on with you to rejoin Alf."

For a heartbeat, everything held: rain, breath, branch. Ellen felt the universe lean toward a choice.

Louisa opened her hands.

The branch dropped, thudding onto the space where Ellen had been sitting seconds before. Bark burst; wet leaves scattered. The sound chased itself down the slope and found an echo, as if the rocks approved of the physics.

Ellen sagged against her friends, blinking hard. When she looked up, the figure had already started to unravel at the edges, red hair blurring into rain, trousers softening into the idea of cloth. Louisa's mouth moved one last time; the whisper rode the air as if carried in a cupped hand.

"He's lost," it said. "Find him."

Then she was gone—no slow fade, just a decision to not be here, the way some people left a room without a sound.

They stood a long moment, three women breathing like runners at the finish line. The rain returned to being only rain.

Sue found her voice first. "Well," she said, but added nothing more.

"What do you think she meant?" Tanya asked before repeating, "He's lost. Find him."

"Do we know how Sawyer died?" Ellen wondered, still leaning on Sue.

"He outlived Alf, but I'm not sure for how long," Sue replied. "Let's get you back to the car and out of this rain, and we'll figure out what to do next."

They moved slowly. The woods seemed to breathe with them, a calmer rhythm now, as if a storm had found its way past. At the top of the path, Ellen paused and looked back.

"We'll find him," she said softly, more vow than speech. "We'll find Sawyer."

Tanya tightened her grip around Ellen's waist. "Let's get you to a doctor first."

"I'm fine," Ellen insisted. "My ankle needs ice and elevation, that's all. And I need out of these wet and muddy clothes."

They started toward the car, three figures threaded together, carrying their equipment and each other, the rain rinsing stone and leaf and story alike. Behind them, Murder Rocks watched them go. Ellen imagined a boy's shape hovering between trees and river, not ready to be seen, not ready to be gone.

She set her jaw and took the next step.

CHAPTER SEVENTEEN

Beneath the Highest Rock

The entrance to the cave looked darker than Ellen remembered. It occurred to her that it was a different entrance to the one Jason Albright had stood before. Shadows thickened in the mouth of the stone like smoke that couldn't quite decide which way to drift. Her breath puffed visibly, though it wasn't cold. Behind her, Sue's and Tanya's voices echoed off the limestone walls as they unpacked their gear.

"Battery check?" Sue called.

"Full," Tanya answered. "At least someone's ready for this."

Ellen didn't respond. Something had snagged her attention—the faintest melody weaving out from the cave's interior, soft and feminine, impossibly distant yet clear as a whisper next to her ear. A lullaby, maybe. Or a prayer.

No—she recognized it. The French nursery rhyme she learned as a child and taught to her kids when they were little.

Frère Jacques, Frère Jacques,

Dormez-vous? Dormez-vous?

Sonnez les matines! Sonnez les matines!

Ding, dang, dong. Ding, dang, dong.

The song floated like smoke from deep within the cave, the words soft but deliberate, wrapped in a haunting echo that prickled Ellen's scalp. She frowned, listening harder.

"Do you hear that?" she whispered.

"Hear what?" Tanya asked, straightening from her equipment bag.

"The song. Someone's singing."

Sue cocked her head. "Ellen, that's just the wind. The tunnels do weird things to it."

"It's not the wind." Ellen's voice was certain now, trembling with conviction. She grabbed the Mini Maglite from her vest pocket and switched it on. The thin beam cut a narrow path through the gloom.

"Ellen—" Sue's warning came too late. Ellen had already ducked under the low arch and stepped inside.

The air changed immediately—cooler, denser, carrying the metallic tang of wet stone. Her light wavered across uneven walls, catching veins of quartz like threads of glass. The song continued, clearer now, winding deeper into the twisting passage.

"Louisa?" Ellen called softly, noticing for the first time that her ankle wasn't bothering her.

That's weird, she thought.

The singing didn't falter. It bounced off the stone in a pattern both soothing and eerie, as if the voice belonged to the rock itself.

"Ellen!" Tanya's voice echoed behind her, faint and alarmed. "Don't go so far in! Wait!"

But Ellen couldn't. The melody drew her forward. Each verse echoed a little farther ahead, luring her through a labyrinth of turns until her flashlight caught a flash of color—*red*, vivid and alive, like a flame glimpsed through fog.

Red hair.

Her heart leapt. "Louisa?"

The figure ahead didn't answer, just moved—a ripple of red hair vanishing around a bend. The song picked up again, its rhythm unbroken, its voice sweet and distant.

Ellen followed, pulse quickening. "Louisa, please! We're trying to help you!"

Her foot slid on a patch of damp clay, but she caught herself against the wall and kept going. The tunnel widened suddenly into a larger chamber. Her beam swept across the space and stopped.

A pile of rocks loomed in the center, fresh and jagged compared to the smooth walls. The ceiling above it sagged, cracked and heavy, the collapse frozen mid-fall as though time itself had been startled.

Ellen's breath came fast. "Oh my God," she whispered.

The song lingered—softer now, almost like a memory of sound. Then Louisa appeared beside the rock pile, her outline pale and translucent, her red hair bright even in the dim light. She stood barefoot, still wearing men's trousers and a simple linen shirt. Her lips moved with the next line of the song—*Dormez-vous?*—and repeated the line, like a scratched vinyl record, her eyes fixed on Ellen. Then, she pointed a ghostly finger at the rubble.

"Is that where Sawyer is?" Ellen asked, her voice barely audible.

Louisa didn't stop singing, but she nodded—once, slowly. Then, mid-verse, her image flickered, thinned, and vanished.

Ellen gasped, her flashlight wobbling. "Louisa!" The beam shook as her hand trembled. "Wait—come back!"

No answer—just the steady drip of water somewhere in the dark.

Ellen's pulse thudded in her ears. She turned, ready to retrace her steps—only to find the tunnel behind her sealed in shadow. For an instant, she thought she saw movement in that blackness: small, slight, the outline of a boy crouched behind the fallen stone.

"Sawyer?" she whispered.

The darkness inhaled.

Ellen jerked awake.

She blinked in the darkness, disoriented by the abrupt return of warmth, color, and ordinary sound. A heater whirred softly. The familiar shape of the Branson condo swam into focus—the twin beds, the pale curtains and blinds separated by a moonbeam. Sue snored softly on the other bed, one arm flung over her face.

Ellen pressed a hand to her chest. Her heart was still galloping, her skin damp with sweat. The echo of the song still clung to her mind—clear, insistent.

Dormez-vous? Dormez-vous?

She turned toward her nightstand, grabbed the notepad and pen she kept there for ideas, and began to write in the dim light of the moon before the dream could dissolve.

Her handwriting shook, looping unevenly across the page. When she set the pen down, she stared at the notes, half expecting them to fade.

Outside, a light rain tapped against the window. Ellen rolled onto her back and closed her eyes, trying to rest, but the melody refused to leave her.

Dormez-vous? Dormez-vous?

She reached for her phone and used Google translate for *Dormez-vous* and gasped at the result: *Are you sleeping?*

Stunned, she turned onto her side, pillow clutched under her chin, and listened to Sue's rhythmic breathing across the room. There was comfort in that sound, along with the hum of her noisemaker—a tether to reality—but the nursery rhyme's cadence threaded through it like an undercurrent, steady and strange.

By the time she finally drifted into a shallow sleep, the song had turned from a haunting into a heartbeat.

The smell of coffee drew Ellen from her bed sometime after nine. Her ankle throbbed as soon as she stood, a dull reminder of yesterday's fall. She slipped on her robe, limped toward the kitchen, and found Sue and Tanya already seated at the small kitchen table, still in pajamas, each with a steaming mug in hand.

"Morning, sunshine," Tanya said with mock brightness. "You look like I feel."

Sue smirked. "She looks like someone who stayed up talking to ghosts all night."

"Close," Ellen muttered, easing into the empty chair as Tanya poured her a cup of coffee. "I dreamed about one." She took the steaming mug. "Thanks."

Her friends leaned forward, eyes alert in an instant. Ellen took a sip of coffee before continuing, the caffeine steadying her voice.

When she'd finished her story, Tanya made a face. "Creepy."

Sue exchanged a glance with Tanya. "You think she was trying to tell you something?"

"It felt like a message, yeah," Ellen confirmed. "Like she wanted me to *see* that spot. I wrote it down right after I woke."

Tanya tilted her head, thoughtful. "That's interesting," she said slowly. "Because I had a dream, too."

Ellen straightened her back. "You did?"

Tanya nodded, setting down her bagel. "In mine, I wasn't me— I was a boy, maybe fifteen, carrying a lantern through the caves. I felt sad and nervous. Then the ground started shaking, rocks falling from everywhere. I tried to run, but the tunnel collapsed. Everything went black, and I woke up gasping. I didn't think anything of it until just now, when I heard your dream. It could be a coincidence, but I don't know. Do you think I was Sawyer?"

Sue's brows lifted. "Yes. The ghosts are trying to tell us something."

"I agree," Ellen said after taking a sip of coffee. "I think he was going after the treasure when the cave collapsed."

Sue sipped her coffee, thoughtful. "It would make sense. Maybe he heard Alf had died and thought he could claim it for himself—or keep it safe."

Ellen nodded slowly. "That fits. Alf mentioned in his letter that the treasure was buried beneath the highest rock. If Sawyer went looking for it, and the caves collapsed there . . ." she trailed off, thinking.

"Then that's where he died," Sue finished softly.

For a long moment, none of them spoke. The hum of the refrigerator filled the silence.

Finally, Ellen straightened. "If we could compare old photographs of Murder Rocks, maybe we could find where the highest point used to be. The terrain changed after the cave-in, but if we find the difference, maybe that's where we can find Sawyer's remains. Maybe he needs a proper burial to move on."

"And maybe the treasure's there, too," Sue added, her eyes gleaming.

Tanya perked up. "Wait a second!" She jumped up from the table and hurried to the living room. "Woody P. Snow's *Murder Rocks*! It's full of historical photos."

"That's right!" Ellen called excitedly.

Tanya returned a moment later, the book in hand, its pages bristling with sticky notes from earlier research. She plopped down beside Sue and began flipping rapidly through the pages. "Okay, here—look at this one." She stabbed her finger at a grainy black-and-white photograph labeled *Murder Rocks, circa 1860*. The formation in the background rose dramatically higher than the one they'd seen. "See? That ridge doesn't exist anymore. It must've collapsed."

Ellen leaned closer, squinting. "That does look different."

"Let's compare," Sue said, pulling her laptop toward her. Within seconds, she had modern images of Murder Rocks on-screen. "All right, side by side."

Tanya angled the book. "Here. Look at the slope of this boulder line."

Ellen pointed to the screen. "And here—it's gone. Completely flattened."

Sue tapped a key, switching angles. "There! You're right. That must be the collapse site."

Tanya grinned. "We found it."

Ellen smiled faintly, though the image of her dream's rock pile pulsed in her mind. "I think Louisa showed me this place."

Sue blew out a slow breath, then glanced toward Ellen's wrapped ankle. "How are you supposed to hike down there again?"

"I'll manage."

"I'm not digging up those rocks by myself," Tanya objected. "Maybe you could hire Caleb and his crew."

Sue shook her head. "We can't risk it. They're nice enough now, but they could turn on us if we found the treasure."

"True," Ellen agreed. You never knew what greed would do to people.

"We'd likely end up in a hole next to Sawyer," Tanya muttered as she sank in her chair.

Sue leaned back. "Although I do have my—"

"No gun," Ellen said automatically.

"No gun," Tanya echoed.

Sue sighed, hands up in mock surrender. "Fine. I won't use my gun. So how exactly do we dig through a rockslide?"

Ellen smiled, the answer already forming. "Who do we call when we need to identify remains? Who cares more about anthropological research and publications than treasure?"

Sue grinned. "Bob Brooks."

Ellen nodded. "Exactly. If anyone can get us clearance to excavate legally—and discreetly—it's him."

Tanya raised her mug in a toast. "To Bob Brooks—the man who prefers femurs to fortune."

They clinked their coffee cups together, laughter easing the tension.

Ellen leaned back in her chair, her tiredness catching up to her. The melody of *Frère Jacques* still hummed faintly in her memory, looping in the background of her thoughts. She glanced out the window at the slate-gray sky. Somewhere under those same clouds, beneath those same rocks, a boy's spirit was still waiting.

CHAPTER EIGHTEEN

Ground Truth

Ellen reached for her phone, the last notes of *Frère Jacques* still echoing somewhere in the back of her mind. She scrolled to *Bob Brooks* and hit call.

He answered on the second ring. "Bob here."

"Hi, Bob. It's Ellen—with Sue and Tanya on speaker. The Ghost Healers? It's been a while."

"Well, now, if it isn't my favorite trio of trouble." His voice held a smile. "Tell me what hole you want me to look into and whether I'll need a bigger shovel."

"We think we found a nineteenth-century collapse site at Murder Rocks near Branson, Missouri," Ellen said. "Possible human remains connected to the Alf Bolin story—a fourteen or fifteen-year-old male known only as Sawyer. There's also a possibility of Civil War treasure. We'll give you a cut if you can come tomorrow. And you'd be welcome to study the remains and write your paper, but we want to give the remains a proper burial as soon as possible. They belong to a vengeful spirit who's already killed one man."

"Killed a man, holy hell," he said. "Murder Rocks . . . is that on public property?"

"Not yet," Sue cut in. "I recently acquired it. The land belongs to me."

"That makes this process a whole lot easier," he said with a sigh. "And Civil Wat treasure? How sure are you?"

"Eighty-five percent," Ellen said, giving her friends a shrug. "Gold and silver bars and Union supplies."

"Send me a pin drop and any historic imagery you've got, and I'll get on the next plane out. I'll text you once I know my ETA."

Ellen clapped her hands. "Thanks, Bob! Looking forward to seeing you."

"Likewise, Ellen. I'll see you ladies soon."

He hung up. The room exhaled.

Tanya snapped into motion. "I'll print the photo plates from Snow's book and the modern angles we found."

Sue shouldered the gear bag. "I'll charge all the equipment and install new batteries where needed."

Ellen sat back in her chair. "I'll ice my ankle. I'm not letting y'all go without me, so I may need a cane, too."

Tuesday dawned crisp and clear, the sky a seamless blue stretched taut above the Victorian. Ellen leaned on a cane beside the Chevy Onix outside, while Sue and Tanya checked in with Caleb and his crew.

The sound of approaching tires on the gravel drew Ellen's attention. A beige pickup truck pulled into the turnout, its bed loaded with equipment cases, coiled cables, and something that looked like a folded stretcher. Behind the wheel, Bob Brooks grinned out at her, his white beard gleaming in the sun.

Tanya and Sue emerged from the Victorian in time to greet him.

"Well, look at you three!" he said as he climbed down. "I swear, every time I see you, you're either in a haunted house or on hallowed ground."

Sue laughed and hugged him. "It's good to see you, Bob."

"Likewise." He exchanged hugs all around as he asked, "Now, which patch of cursed dirt are we investigating today?" He grabbed a case from the bed of his rental pickup while the ladies grabbed their gear.

"It's not far," Sue replied.

After slinging their bags over their shoulders, Ellen and her friends guided Bob along the trail, relaying what had happened to Jason Albright and describing their own near-death experiences. They told him what they knew about Alf, Louisa, and Sawyer, explaining the dreams, the historical photos, the probable collapse site. Bob listened without interrupting, his blue eyes sharp beneath bushy brows. When they reached Murder Rocks, where the limestone rose in pale slabs, he stopped and took a slow look around.

"Well, I'll be," he murmured. "You ladies weren't kidding. Even from here, I can see that's a classic cave-in formation. See how the slope changes there?" He pointed with a gloved hand. "Nature's version of a scar."

Ellen followed his gaze to a flattened collection of rocks. She'd seen it from a different vantage point in her dream—underground. Her stomach tightened.

Bob set down his equipment case and popped it open. Inside, neatly nested in foam, were an array of compact instruments: a tablet computer, coiled sensors, a radar antenna shaped like a small sled. He patted it affectionately. "Meet Mabel. She's old, cranky, and hates rain, but she can see through rock better than Superman."

Sue whistled softly. "You travel with quite the entourage."

"Every scientist needs his toys." Bob grinned. "And this is so much easier to travel with than that lawn mower of a machine I used in Tulsa. Remember?"

The three ladies laughed. That seemed like a lifetime ago.

"Now, before we play, tell me exactly what the ghosts said."

Ellen hesitated, feeling slightly foolish. "Louisa showed me—well, *dreamed* me—a pile of rocks. She nodded when I asked if Sawyer was there. I followed her through that entrance there."

It wasn't the same entrance that Jason Albright had stood near when he'd broadcast his final video. It looped around the back and presented as a tighter hole.

"Dreams," Bob mused, uncoiling a cable. "Half the good archaeology in the world starts with dreams. Or dumb luck."

Tanya shrugged. "We'll take either."

"Lead the way," he said to Ellen.

She grabbed her headlamp from her bag and strapped it on, Sue and Tanya following suit.

"You ladies are prepared," Bob praised as he pulled a Mini Maglite from his trouser pocket.

"This isn't our first rodeo," Sue reminded him.

"Indeed, it's not," he said with a laugh.

Using her cane, Ellen ducked through the small entrance, following the serpentine tunnel, just as she had in her dream. She half-expected to hear the French nursery rhyme ahead.

"It's a good thing I'm not claustrophobic," Sue said. "Or am I? I can't remember."

"You aren't, but I am," Tanya called from behind her.

"Just remember to breathe," Bob encouraged from the rear.

After a few more turns, the tunnel opened up into a wide chamber, just as it had in Ellen's dream, and there before them was the pile of rocks, lying as they had for more than a century. They appeared immovable, like they'd cemented together over the years.

"There," Ellen pointed, just as Louisa had.

Somewhere, Ellen though she heard someone singing, *Dormez-vous? Dormez-vous?*

Bob worked for nearly an hour, the hum of the GPR unit sounding just like a nursery rhyme. He moved methodically, guiding the radar sled in slow passes over the collapse site, while Sue, Tanya, and Ellen found knee-high boulders to sit on and tried to talk to ghosts. They were quiet today, the spirit box only a shuffling cadence with no intelligible words.

Finally, Bob crouched beside the monitor. "Well, would you look at that," he murmured.

Ellen limped closer. On the tablet's display, faint bands of color rippled through the cross-section of the earth—yellow, green, blue. But one shape stood out: an elongated oval, maybe five feet long, with a density contrast different from the surrounding stone.

"What is it?" Sue asked.

"An anomaly," Bob said softly. "Could be a void, could be a cavity, or it could be what you came here for."

Ellen's breath hitched. "Sawyer."

"Possibly," Bob said. "This shape here looks like an intact human skull."

Ellen and her friends exchanged looks of excitement.

"And there's something else." Bob tapped a smaller cluster of signals beside it—metallic reflections forming sharp, irregular lines. "Those might be artifacts—metal, maybe wood fragments."

"The treasure?" Tanya asked.

"Could be," he said.

They all stared at the monitor, silence settling over them. The temperature dropped noticeably—enough that Ellen saw her breath.

Bob rubbed his arms. "Well, that's interesting."

"What is?" Sue asked.

He nodded toward the equipment. "Static interference. Field's spiking."

The radar sled emitted a sudden high-pitched whine, then went dead. The monitor flickered. Ellen glanced around—the light seemed to dim, the colors flattening into shades of gray.

"Bob?" she asked carefully.

He frowned, tapping the machine. "Don't worry. Happens sometimes with mineral interference."

But Ellen knew better. The shift in the air was too familiar, too specific. She'd felt it before every manifestation they'd ever encountered.

Then came the voice, a whisper that was above and below them at the same time: "Don't dig."

All four of them froze.

Bob's head jerked up. "Who said that?"

Ellen swallowed hard. "You heard it?"

"Of course I heard it." Bob's eyes widened. "And I believe that makes me officially on board with your haunting."

The voice came again, louder this time, trembling with grief and fury. "Don't dig!"

A cold gust surged through the cavern in a place where no wind should enter. The hair on Ellen's arms rose.

"Bob," she said quietly, "pack up the equipment. We need to step back."

He didn't argue. Together they packed Mabel back into her case.

Bob exhaled slowly. "Well," he said, voice shaking only a little, "that's the first time a ghost has yelled at me."

Ellen managed a weak smile. "Welcome to our world."

Tanya's eyes were bright with adrenaline. "That was Sawyer. He's trying to stop us."

"Maybe," Ellen said.

"Well, I can tell you one thing for sure: something human is buried under that rock. I'll file a preliminary report with the county and request an archaeological permit. Once we have that, we can excavate safely."

"And if Sawyer doesn't want us to?" Sue asked.

Bob met her gaze. "Then you'll have to do what you always do—convince him it's time to let go."

Ellen turned toward the mound again, heart pounding. The air above it shimmered faintly, as though heat rose from the stone despite the chill.

"We will," she whispered. "We will."

C H A P T E R   N I N E T E E N

Footfalls and Forewarnings

The trail out of Murder Rocks seemed steeper to Ellen. She leaned hard on the cane she'd bought at Walmart, the rubber tip tapping a staccato counterpoint to the crunch of gravel underfoot. Two paces ahead, Tanya and Sue carried their packs of equipment over their shoulders. Bob brought up the rear at first, then strode ahead to point out a fault line in the rock, his voice low and cheerful.

They had all heard it in the chamber—the voice like air squeezed through teeth: *Don't dig.* Back on the surface, the world looked too bright for warnings, even below the thick canopy of leaves. Sunlight had washed away last night's rain, making everything glitter.

Then she heard the footfalls.

Not the echo of their own procession, not a twig surrendering to the weight of a squirrel. This was soft and human and exactly one beat late—like a child stepping where your heel had just been. Ellen stopped and turned, cane sinking a half inch into damp grit.

"Hello?" she called, voice carrying and then coming back to her. "Is someone there?"

Sue and Tanya turned first, then Bob, whose blue eyes narrowed as he shaded them with one hand. The trail behind them curved and fell away, swallowed by scrub oak and dogwood. Sunlight flashed and died in the greens. Nothing moved.

"Bill?" Sue called, voice sharpening. "If that's you, you're trespassing."

Ellen listened. The woods listened back.

She heard it again, this time to the right, below the trail—a muffled shift, like a boot testing a patch of leaf-mold, then withdrawing.

"Over there," Ellen said, gesturing with the cane.

Bob set Mabel's waterproof case more securely on his shoulder. "Let's take a look," he said mildly, as if suggesting a detour for wildflowers. "Nice and slow."

"Could be a bear," Tanya warned.

Ellen shook her head. "It sounded like a boot."

Sue took the lead, eyes scanning in a sweep pattern like she was tracking a lost toddler at a fairground. Tanya fell in beside Ellen, close enough to catch her if the ankle wobbled. The four of them left the trail together and descended the shallow slope, bracken whispering against their jeans. A breeze stirred, cool and crisp after yesterday's rain, and Ellen wrapped her scarf more tightly around her neck before continuing down the path.

"Hey!" Sue called suddenly, crouching. She held up a scrap of burlap snagged on a low cedar branch. Fresh fibers frayed and clung like a shed snakeskin.

Ellen's stomach tightened. "Bill Kirby—or another treasure hunter, I suppose."

"Could be a game hunter," Bob suggested, though his face said he didn't believe it. "Or somebody hauling deer feed."

"No one should be in these woods," Sue said loud enough to be heard all the way down at Murder Rocks.

They fanned out. Ellen moved carefully, eyes scanning the forest floor, taking in the mirco-narratives: cloven deer tracks pressed into soft earth, the scribble of a raccoon's hands along a washout, a scatter of walnuts cracked by teeth hard as tools. Nothing like a boot print—not in obvious outline. Whoever had followed them knew how to step in shadow and on old rock, leaving more suggestion than mark.

"Ellen." Tanya's voice lowered to a murmur. She pointed at a patch of disturbed leaf litter beneath a hackberry stump. Someone had crouched here recently; the leaves showed two shallow knee impressions and the faint oval from something set down—a canteen? a camera?

Ellen's pulse jumped in her throat. She straightened slowly, cane anchoring her. "All right," she said, addressing trees and ghosts and trespassers alike, "enough. If you're Louisa or Sawyer, you've had our attention since day one. If you're Bill Kirby, you're trespassing. Show yourself."

The woods did what woods do—kept their counsel.

Bob squinted downslope. "I don't love us wandering off trail with a possible tail," he said gently. "If we spook a real person, we've got a different problem than etiquette with the dead."

"Don't worry, Bob," Sue intoned. "I've got my gun."

Tanya and Ellen rolled their eyes.

"Back to the path," Ellen insisted. "Let's get out of here."

Tanya led the way. "You don't have to tell me twice."

They climbed, Ellen testing each step, the ache in her ankle a constant chastisement. At the trail again, she couldn't shake it—the feeling of being measured by someone just out of sight. A second footfall echoed, this time directly behind them and closer. She whirled faster than her ankle liked. Pain flared; she bit back a yelp.

"Ellen?" Sue reached for her.

"I heard it," Ellen said, breath thin. "Right there."

Bob's jaw flexed. He cupped his hands around his mouth. "If you're a hunter or hiker," he called, "announce yourself. We don't want anyone hurt."

For a heartbeat, nothing. Then—a sound, unmistakable this time: a quick inhale, the small shock of someone realizing they've been caught listening. A bird burst from a shrub in a scatter of wings. Leaves rustled as if something passed through them.

Tanya turned, every line of her suddenly alert. She stared at the empty stretch of trail behind them, then at each of their faces. "That wasn't just me, right?"

"Right," Ellen said softly. The hair along her arms rose. "Louisa?" She called for the ghost even though her gut told her it was something else.

"Let's get back to the house," Sue suggested. "I'm out of breath, and I need to pee."

"Me, too," Tanya said.

The pressure eased, the way a crowded room softens when the person you've been waiting for arrives. Somewhere far below, a creek resumed its ordinary babbling. Bob shifted Mabel's case and let out a breath he pretended was from exertion.

"I believe you ladies owe me a tour of this famous Victorian."

They finally emerged from the woods and followed the path from the back to the front of the house, where Bob's beige truck sat, sun flashing along the ladder rack. Bob lifted Mabel gently, as if she were a child, and slid her into place, securing the straps with practiced hands.

"Good girl," he murmured to the machine, then to the three of them: "All right. Are you going to show me the house, or what?"

Caleb met them on the wraparound porch, pencil behind his ear and a ring of paint on one knuckle. He grinned at Bob now, offering a paint-speckled hand. "Caleb Rivera."

Bob shook, eyes taking in the restored corbels, the turned balusters, the faint sway in the porch boards that said original and proud. "Bob Brooks."

They stepped inside. Afternoon light laid a cathedral hush over the stairwell. The salt line they'd laid days ago had been scuffed by boots and the rolling of a tool chest; Ellen's eyes went to it immediately, a reflex she wished she didn't have. The line was broken near the newel. Tanya noticed, too.

Bob drifted into the parlor as if drawn by a magnet. "These mantels are original," he said, fingers hovering respectfully over the marble. "See the veining? Local quarry, probably. Late 1890s pattern."

Sue preened the way you do when an expert declares your child talented. "We thought so," she said. "What about the medallions?"

"Also original," Bob said. "And in fine condition." He leaned close to the crown molding where the painters had taped off a crisp line. "Hand-tooled. Those tiny irregularities are a craftsman's heartbeat."

Ellen loved him a little for that—the way he could find a person in the work.

Caleb gestured toward the dining room. "We found an old wallpaper fragment behind the built-in. Turn-of-the-century floral. Sue's thinking of matching it for the upper half of the wall, paint below. Balance the room."

Bob nodded. "Great idea, Sue."

"I hear that a lot."

Tanya and Ellen rolled their eyes while the men chuckled.

They moved room to room, continuing upstairs. Bob confirmed that the doors and knobs were original, and some of the windows, too. He was pleased by the historical details, which, in turn, pleased Sue.

A clatter erupted downstairs—hard, sudden—followed by the pitched oath of a man surprised by gravity. Everyone flinched.

Caleb swore and hurried down. Sue was on his heel, then Tanya. Ellen tried to follow at their pace and her ankle caught. Bob slowed beside her, steadying her elbow without making a fuss of it.

"I'm fine," she managed, breath clipping. "Go."

They reached the first floor to find chaos in the dining room—a toppled ladder splayed like a drunk praying mantis, a paint tray facedown in a gray pond, and a man on the floor clutching his forearm, teeth bared in a pain, like he was trying to be brave. Another painter hovered, eyes wide, hands open and useless.

"What happened?" Caleb demanded. He swept the fallen roller aside and pressed two fingers gently to the man's wrist. "Can you move your fingers?"

"Barely," the painter grunted through his jaw. "Hurts like—" He glanced at Ellen and swallowed the rest. "Like blazes."

"Did the ladder slip?" Sue asked, scanning the floor for slick spots. "Did your shoe catch?"

The uninjured painter shook his head so hard his cap nearly flung itself across the room. "No. I saw it. The ladder jumped."

Caleb shot him a look. "Ladders don't jump."

The injured painter stared at the ceiling, breathing through his nose. "Something pushed it."

"And it wasn't me," the uninjured painter insisted.

Silence widened in the hallway like a spill. The women had heard those words before. In halls like this. In houses like this.

"Okay," Caleb said after a beat, voice even but tight. "Sam, go get the kit," he said to the uninjured painter. "We'll need to splint this."

Bob crouched on the other side. "I can stabilize until you get him to urgent care," he said. He wrapped the forearm with practiced efficiency, improvising with a clean rag and a ruler Tanya handed over from nowhere, like a magician's assistant.

Ellen moved to the base of the fallen ladder. Her cane tip nudged one of the spreader bars. No paint slick beneath. The feet had been rubbered and clean. She looked at the wall. The pattern in the dripped gray trim ran in lines like rainfall on the royal blue walls. She could see the moment the ladder went, the man's hand grabbing for air that did not hold.

"I don't like this," Sue said softly, voice pitched only for Ellen and Tanya.

"Me neither," Tanya said. "I think Sawyer's back in the house, even angrier now that he knows we plan to dig."

Ellen's scalp prickled. "I think you may be right. Maybe it was him following us in the woods."

"All right," Sue said to Caleb, "we need to halt all work on this house until after the excavation." She turned to Ellen. "We're going to salt and burn those bones if it's the last thing I do."

Sue was shaking with anger.

"Take a deep breath," Ellen urged her.

A hush rippled. If a house can hold its breath, this one did.

"How long before you get that permit?" Tanya asked Bob.

"I'll call in some favors. Maybe as early as Friday."

Sue turned back to Caleb. "Don't plan to return before Monday. I'll keep you in the loop."

"Let's clean up this mess," Caleb said to his men. "We're out of here until further notice." Then he turned to the injured painter, who was now on his feet holding his hurt wrist. "Jerry, you wait in the truck. I'll take you to the ER as soon as we're done here."

Jerry let out a tight laugh that had pain in it but also relief. "Thank you," he said.

In the foyer, Tanya discretely refreshed the salt line with a quick dash from her tote, her movements small and ordinary as a woman applying perfume. She waggled the shaker at Ellen; the two of them shared a look that said, *Better safe than sorry.*

CHAPTER TWENTY

The Unearthing

By Friday morning—two weeks after Ellen, Sue, and Tanya had first arrived in Branson—the permits had come through, thanks to Bob's reputation with the Missouri Historical Preservation Office. He'd spent the evening on the phone, charming bureaucrats with the kind of affable persistence only an elderly academic could manage.

Now, in the cool shadow of Murder Rocks, he crouched beside the flagged perimeter, checking the ground-penetrating radar's calibration while Ellen, Sue, and Tanya unloaded shovels, crowbars, buckets, and the smaller trowels Bob had brought down the trail in a wheelbarrow.

Ellen adjusted her hard hat—Bob had insisted they all wear one—and was grateful that her ankle was stronger today. Although she walked without the cane as she carried a crowbar, trowel, and shovel, she found herself using the shovel to bear some of her weight.

The secondary entrance to the caves yawned like a mouth in the hillside, its edges bearded with moss and shadows. A rope of LED lanterns—Bob's idea—snaked inside, throwing weak pools of light onto slick rock. Ellen followed close behind him, her flat-heeled boots, along with the edge of her shovel, crunching against gravel.

Except for what she carried, the dream had begun exactly like this—same air, same echo, same uneasy melody whispering through stone. But this time, Louisa's song didn't come.

Sue's headlamp beam swung across a low wall of rubble ahead. The tunnel opened into a larger cavern where fractured limestone arched above them like the ribs of an ancient beast. In the center, the collapse rose in a mound of rock and clay—a jagged cairn at least six feet high.

"We're back," Ellen announced playfully to the ghosts, trying to lighten the mood.

Bob was already unpacking his instruments. "If Sawyer's here, we'll find him."

He crouched beside his ground-penetrating radar sled—Mabel, as he called it—and began guiding it in slow, careful passes over the mound. The faint hum of electronics filled the chamber, mingling with the drip of groundwater.

"Signal's good," he murmured. "If I remember correctly, should be about here."

The rest of them stayed back, letting him work.

Bob's monitor flickered. "There you are."

With deliberate care, Bob pried at the stones on the upper slope with a crowbar. The others followed suit, moving rock by rock, bucket by bucket. Dust filled the air, catching in their throats. Every so often the cave gave a soft groan, a reminder of its fragility.

Hours passed in the dank and musty cave. Ellen had begun to sweat despite the cold but continued to help even though the others had warned her to rest her ankle.

Then Sue gasped. "Here—look!"

Ellen crouched beside her. The tip of a boot had emerged from the soil—leather shrunken and fused with bone. Nearby lay a rusted buckle and the faint outline of a hand curled around something round and dull.

Bob brushed gently. "Brass locket," he said, voice hushed. "He must've carried it until the end."

Ellen wondered if it had once contained photos of Sawyer's parents. He'd been on the orphan train from New York, but she knew nothing about what had put him there.

The earth seemed to sigh. A thin breeze, impossible underground, brushed her cheek.

Ellen knelt beside Bob as he brushed away debris. Half-buried in the soil was the unmistakable curve of another human bone—delicate but unmistakable.

"Femur," he murmured. "Juvenile. Maybe fifteen or sixteen."

"It really is Sawyer," Ellen whispered as she met the smiles of her friends.

Bob nodded solemnly. "Looks like you were right."

They uncovered more—ribs, the slope of a skull, fragments of cloth. The air grew colder, and now that she was no longer laboring, Ellen was chilled.

"Do you feel that?" Sue asked.

Tanya glanced around the cavern. "He's watching."

Bob straightened, sweat streaking his temple. "We'll document this and get a full team in here. But for now—"

He tapped the side of the mound where the radar had pinged. "Let's clear this section. There's another cavity here, maybe where the artifacts settled."

They shifted to the new spot, brushing and lifting, their movements automatic and reverent. When Sue's trowel struck wood, the sound echoed unnaturally loud. Together, they cleared a rotted chest from the rubble, its iron bands eaten through with rust. Bob pried the lid open, and a dull gleam spilled out: coins, jewelry, a rusted pistol grip.

Sue exhaled. "Treasure. I bet there's more."

Tanya looked around nervously. "I don't think we should—" her voice trailed off.

The cave's air had changed again—denser, vibrating faintly. The hairs on Ellen's arms rose.

"What was that?" Ellen whispered.

Bob frowned. "Barometric shift, maybe. Or—"

A low growl rolled through the cavern, deep as thunder. The lantern light flickered. So did Ellen's headlamp.

"—Or not," Bob finished grimly.

Ellen's pulse spiked. "Sawyer, it's all right," she said to the darkness. "We're here to help you join Alf and Louisa on the other side. This treasure is no longer your responsibility, and it can't do anything for you."

Sue put her hands on her hips, warrior-ready. "My mother used to say that you can't take your toys with you to the grave, but evidently you did. But, Sawyer, it's time to let them go, so we can bury you in a proper grave and you can find your eternal peace."

The growl deepened, turning into a hiss of words that shivered through the walls. *Leave it . . .*

Tanya backed up. "He's angry."

Ellen glanced upward. Pebbles rattled loose from the ceiling. "He's warning us."

Sue lifted her voice, steady but pleading. "Sawyer, you did your duty. You kept your promise to Alf. But he and Louisa are waiting for you. You can rest now."

For a heartbeat, silence. Then another whisper—ragged, almost human: *Don't dig.*

Before anyone could respond, a distant sound echoed from the tunnel behind them—a scuff of boots on stone.

Bob looked up sharply. "You expecting company?"

Ellen shook her head. "No one knows we're here."

But someone did.

A beam of light flashed across the chamber wall, cutting through dust.

"Oh no," Sue breathed. "Not him."

Bob exhaled. "Who is—"

A metallic *click* cut him off.

They froze.

"Now isn't this a fine discovery," said a familiar voice, smooth as oil. "Looks like I showed up just in time."

Bill Kirby stepped into Ellen's circle of light, rifle leveled, eyes glittering with greed, a grin wide and hungry.

"Mr. Kirby," Ellen said carefully. "You shouldn't be here."

"Funny," he said. "I was about to say the same to you."

"This is my property," Sue reminded him. "We have every right to be here, and you're trespassing."

He gestured with the gun. "Step away from the treasure. Nice and easy."

Ellen's jaw tightened. "Have you been following us?"

"For days," he said proudly. "Figured you were chasing more than ghost stories."

Bob straightened, calm but alert. "Sir, this is an archaeological site. You're interfering with a state-sanctioned dig."

Kirby chuckled. "State-sanctioned, huh? You got a badge to go with that beard, Professor?"

Bob didn't flinch. "I've got more ethics than you'll find in that barrel of yours."

"Cute." Kirby waved the rifle toward the treasure. "Now, let's make this simple. You four sit yourselves down, nice and quiet."

When no one moved, he cocked the hammer. "Do it."

They obeyed, each finding a flat boulder to sit on. Bill pulled a coil of rope from his pack—clearly prepared—and began tying their wrists. His hands shook slightly with excitement.

"You've been watching us this whole time," Sue said through gritted teeth.

"Long enough to know you were onto something." He knotted Ellen's wrists. "I followed you last week, right up to the cave mouth. Heard you talking to air. Figured you were crazy until you started hauling in the professor."

Ellen winced as the rope dug into her skin. "You don't know what you're doing, Bill."

"Sure, I do." He crouched beside the trench, eyes gleaming at the open chest, the mounds of coins and jewels. "I'm doing what Alf Bolin should've done—taking what's mine."

"That treasure belongs to this woman, the landowner," Bob said evenly, gesturing toward Sue. "It's hers by law."

Kirby laughed. "I don't think so. I've been searching for this haul for decades. I deserve it more than she does."

Kirby reached in, grabbing handfuls of coins and jewelry, stuffing them into burlap sacks. "But I'm grateful to you, I really am. Couldn't have found it without you and your fancy equipment."

Ellen's heart pounded. "You need to stop. You're provoking him."

"Provoking who?" Kirby sneered. "Your imaginary friends?"

The air around him shimmered. Ellen saw it first—the faint distortion, like heat rising from asphalt. "Mr. Kirby," she whispered. "Please."

He ignored her, laughing as he slung the first sack over his shoulder. "Tell your ghosts thanks for the help."

Then came the growl.

Low at first, deepening until it vibrated through the rocks beneath and above them. Kirby froze. His grin faltered.

"What the hell was that?"

Sue's eyes widened. "That's Sawyer."

The ground trembled—a subtle vibration that sent pebbles dancing. Kirby stumbled, nearly losing his grip on the rifle.

"Earthquake?" he asked, voice breaking.

Bob shook his head. "Not the kind you can measure."

A sudden gust whipped through the cavern, strong enough to scatter dust and lift Kirby's hat clean off his head. The burlap sack ripped open, coins spilling into the trench. The air crackled with static.

"Stop it!" Kirby shouted, aiming his rifle at the air. "You can't scare me!"

But Ellen saw it now—a figure forming behind him, young, slight, eyes like hollow moons. Sawyer. His translucent hand reached for the gun barrel.

The rifle fired—once, wildly. The shot hit the ceiling and ricocheted, and for a terrifying moment, Ellen wondered if someone had been hit. The gun flew from Kirby's hands, spinning end over end before clattering against the rocks.

Kirby staggered back. "Get off me!" He swung blindly, striking only air.

Sawyer's shape brightened, his outline pulsing with light. The ground shuddered again, louder, harder. Spider cracks appeared in the soil near the collapsed cave wall.

"Bill, run!" Ellen shouted. "He's trying to stop you!"

A second later, the ceiling gave way.

The sound was like thunder. Stone and dirt poured down in a blinding cascade. Ellen threw herself sideways, dragging Sue with her. The air filled with dust and the roar of falling rock.

When the world settled, the chamber was half-filled with debris. Kirby was gone—buried beneath the mound he'd tried to steal. The gun lay crushed near the broken chest, coins scattered like dull stars across the rubble.

Sawyer's ghost vanished.

Ellen whispered, "You protected it, Sawyer. You can rest now."

"That ceiling might still be unstable," Bob warned as he strained against the rope. "We need to get out and give it time to stabilize."

Ellen pulled her wrists apart, but the rope wouldn't budge.

"If only I could reach my phone," Sue said in a desperate plea.

"Almost there," Tanya said, offering a light of hope to the team, as she wriggled her wrists free. "There."

"Bless, you," Sue said with tears in her eyes. "I was beginning to think we'd be trapped in here with Sawyer and Kirby for all eternity."

Tanya untied the others with trembling hands.

Bob immediately crouched beside the rocks, checking for movement from Kirby, but it was useless. No one could have survived that downpour of rock.

As she took up her bag, Tanya said softly, "Sawyer saved us."

"He saved *the treasure*," Ellen argued. "I don't think he cares about *us*."

They gathered their things in the cavern, breathing dust, four survivors. The treasure glimmered faintly among the rubble—coins dulled by dust, relics of greed and grief alike.

"Let's get out of here and call the authorities," Bob said, gesturing for the ladies to lead the way.

As Tanya turned to go, she said, "Thank you, Sawyer."

CHAPTER TWENTY-ONE

Official Business

Deputy Colton answered on the second ring.

"Colton."

"It's Ellen McManius," Ellen said, keeping her voice steady. "We need to report a death at Murder Rocks."

A pause, then the sound of a chair scraping. "Say that again."

She did, carefully, without the parts that would put a ghost in the record. She told him Bill Kirby had followed them underground, that he'd pulled a gun, that a shot fired and the ceiling came down. She did not say that a boy made of light had reached for the barrel. She said what the living could swallow.

"Where are you now?" Colton asked.

"The trailhead behind the Victorian. Meet us here, and we'll guide you down."

He clicked his tongue, a habit she remembered from the death of Jason Albright—the habit of a man measuring which gear to shift. "All right. Be there in ten."

The line went dead. Ellen stared at her reflection on the dark screen for a second longer before tucking her phone into her pocket. Behind her, in the late afternoon, the Murder Rocks path disappeared into cedars as if the earth had inhaled and closed its mouth.

Sue pressed a water bottle into Ellen's hands. "Drink," she said gently. "You sound like a flight attendant in a storm."

Tanya managed a quick smile that didn't quite land. "Which makes me the person in seat 12C asking if the people near the emergency exits are qualified."

Bob leaned against the tailgate of his rental truck, arms folded, the beam of the weak sun turning his white beard to frost. "Law first," he said quietly. "Then bones."

They didn't have to wait long. A county cruiser pulled in behind them, followed by a second. Deputy Colton climbed out—broad-shouldered, hat brim casting his eyes in shade. Reese slid out the passenger side, notepad already in hand.

Colton shook Ellen's hand, then Sue's, then Tanya's, then Bob's. His gaze shifted to the trail. "All right. Led the way."

They led the deputies down the path, then into the hive-mouth opening. As they ducked and trod through the serpentine tunnel—headlamps carving cones of light—Ellen felt each curve and pinch. She kept one palm on the wall, the damp limestone cool and close. The men's radios murmured, their voices slightly too loud in the pocketed silence.

At the choke point before the larger chamber, Colton held up a hand. "Stop. Everyone all right?" He let Reese take the lead with the flashlight, sweeping the beam in slow arcs, absorbing the geometry, the angles of collapse, the recent scar where stone had broken and lay in fresh, pale plates.

They stepped into the cavern.

Even after all the trips in and out over the last week, the place took Ellen's breath away: the big-bellied ceiling (lower now), the dark, wet streaks, the mound of fallen rock in the center like an altar the earth had built for itself. Closer to them, beneath tons of stone, lay Kirby—his body swallowed by the new fall, his presence indicated only by the position where he'd stood and the fragments of what he'd carried. The ruined rifle, a torn scrap of coat, the ripped mouth of a burlap sack. A few coins still winked among dust and rubble.

Reese whistled under his breath, the sound instantly devoured by the room. "Lord."

Colton's eyes flicked over everything, absorbing, sorting. "Nobody touch anything," he said gently.

"Deputy," Bob said, respectful but confident, "the roof's fragile here, but stable for the moment. We mapped the stress lines before the last collapse. If you can secure a small team, I can show you the safest approach to remove him."

"Appreciate that," Colton said without looking away from the scene. "But we'll run point."

"Of course."

Colton turned to Ellen. "Tell me again what happened."

She spoke carefully, tracing their steps from the top—returning after the permit, bringing the equipment, finding the cavity, seeing the bones, opening the box, and the sense of being watched on the trail earlier in the week. She described Kirby stepping into the chamber, his gun raised, rope in his pack. She didn't describe how the temperature fell or how her ears had filled with pressure until she half expected her own blood to ring. She said the gun went off. She said the ceiling gave.

"Did he threaten you?" Colton asked.

"He told us to sit on the floor," Sue said evenly. "He was shaking with excitement. He tied us up. When Ellen tried to reason with him, he laughed."

Reese's pencil scratched. "Did he say why he followed you?"

"He'd been shadowing us for days," Tanya said. "He was a treasure hunter letting others do the hard work for him."

Colton glanced at Bob. "And you?"

"I can confirm their account," Bob said. "I've no interest in dramatizing this. A man walked into a compromised chamber with a loaded weapon. He fired. The shock and vibration likely accelerated an existing failure in the roof."

"Likely," Colton repeated, filing away the careful word.

Bob didn't blink. "The geology was already in motion, Deputy. He created the wrong sound at the wrong time."

Colton collected their statements individually, which meant Ellen stood alone for a few minutes while Sue stepped back toward the tunnel with Reese and the notebook, and Bob crouched near a crack to show Colton a vein of weakness the average lay person might miss. Ellen switched off her headlamp for a moment, letting the deputies' beams do the work. The dark folded around her like a coat.

That was when the room changed.

It started as a thimbleful of cold at her wrist, just above the cuff of her jacket—like someone had poured water inside the sleeve. She looked down instinctively and saw nothing. Then her breath plumed, slow and steady, though the air had been warm enough minutes ago. A faint hush threaded through the chamber, sifting along the stone, gathering without moving air—like the moment before a word.

Ellen lifted her head. "Sawyer?" she said quietly.

Across the mound, a light shifted. It wasn't the deputies' beams; it didn't cut. It glowed—bluish, soft-edged, the shape of a boy drawing itself like a sketch: collarbones first, thin shoulders, a jaw too young to be done with fear. The figure hovered not far from where the chest had been, near the place the locket had been found. The coins on the rubble pinged—a sound too delicate for stone, like someone tapping glass with a fingernail.

"Don't," the light breathed.

Colton turned, catching the peripheral change, and swore under his breath, half-prayer, half reflex. "What was that?" His beam hunted the glow; the glow dissolved under it, then reassembled two feet to the left—like a child avoiding a grown-up's hand.

"Temperature shift," Bob said calmly, as if announcing cloud cover.

"Just now noticed," Reese muttered, rubbing a forearm. "Like a walk-in freezer."

A pebble slid down the slope of the new collapse and ticked into the silence. Ellen felt the prickle in her scalp, the charge in the skin between her shoulder blades. She reached for the scratches at the nape of her neck. "Sawyer, relax. We're not taking anything." *At least, not to-day*, she thought to herself.

The glow flared briefly, then dimmed—uncertain, as if it had a vocabulary of two signs.

Colton's face had gone still. Not disbelief—caution. He scanned the ceiling, then the floor. "This chamber is unstable," he said, voice even but a shade louder than conversation. "I need you to clear out now."

"Of course," Bob said immediately. He set a hand on Ellen's arm to steady her over a spill of gravel. "Deputy's right."

On the way to the tunnel mouth, Colton leaned in close to Bob. "You were planning to dig more."

"Under an archaeological permit, with structural supports," Bob said. "Not like this. Not now."

"You hear that?" Colton angled his head toward the chamber where the glow had been. "That sound? That's rock deciding what story it wants to tell. My job is to keep it from telling it on top of you."

Bob inclined his head. "Understood."

They backed into the tunnel one by one, the cavern's darkness resuming its seat behind them. In the cramped passage, the men's radios crackled with outside voices—calls for a recovery team, a request for EMS staging "just in case," instructions to seal the trailhead until further notice. The chatter felt like city noise jammed into a church. Ellen found herself grateful for it.

When they reached the surface, the afternoon had gone thin and bright, the kind of winter light that makes every edge look newly sharpened. Colton stepped away to confer with the arriving team— ropes and hard hats and quiet competence. Reese took a few photos. Tanya took another drink from her water bottle. Sue stared at the cave mouth and the trees beyond with that squint she got when she was deciding what to do with her power.

Ellen could almost hear Sue's thoughts: *This is my domain.*

Colton returned with a clipboard. "Here's how this goes," he said. "We're going to secure the site. We'll bring in a small team to retrieve Mr. Kirby and his effects. No one goes back in until we clear it."

"Understood," Sue said. "For how long?"

"As long as it takes." He fixed Bob with a look that wasn't unfriendly but left very little wiggle room. "Professor, I strongly recommend you reconsider the dig. Even with supports. That roof's talking."

Bob nodded slowly, weighing words. "I take your recommendation seriously." Then, softer, the educator in him stepping forward: "But I'll also say this, the lost should be found. If we can do that without harm, we should."

Colton's eyes held his for a beat. "Just try not to let anyone else get killed."

A gust rattled the cedars. Somewhere down the slope a bluejay shrieked.

Ellen cleared her throat. "Deputy," she said. "We'll stand back until you're finished. You have my word."

"Good." He tore off a copy of a form and handed it to her. "Here's my card, again. If you remember anything else, call."

Ellen accepted it. "I will."

Reese waved from the cruiser, already on the radio.

Colton tapped his hat. "We'll be in touch."

They watched the deputies and the team move with the choreography of practiced caution—ropes fed, helmets adjusted, voices clipped. When the last helmet bobbed into the dark, the four of them stood together in the chilled light, their breath a makeshift cloud.

Tanya rubbed her arms. "He thinks we're insane," she said, not like a complaint but like a weather report.

"He thinks he's responsible," Sue said.

Bob scraped a hand over his beard. "He isn't wrong about danger."

"We have no choice," Sue insisted. "Colton doesn't understand that, but you do, don't you, Bob?"

Bob nodded once and slung the case containing Mabel over his shoulder. "I could use a drink. What do you say, ladies?"

"Coffee for me," Sue said. "And maybe lunch."

Tanya huffed a laugh. "There's no *maybe* about it. I'm starved."

"I agree," Ellen said. "And I need to get off this ankle for a while."

They emerged from the woods and trekked to their respective vehicles, having decided on Paula Deen's. If they were ever in need of Gooey Butter Cake, it was today.

CHAPTER TWENTY-TWO

The Reckoning

The day after the deputies had completed their recovery, the sky hung low and gray over the Ozarks. Mist beaded the trees and slicked the limestone trail, turning each step into a risky game Ellen hoped she was prepared to play.

Bob led the way, pushing his wheelbarrow full of tools, followed by two of his graduate assistants—a serious young woman named Mel and a broad-shouldered man called Aaron, both earnest, both unaware that archaeology wasn't the only thing waiting for them underground. Sue and Tanya followed, gear slung over their shoulders, their faces pale in the early light.

Ellen brought up the rear, using the cane again, even though her ankle was stronger. She carried nothing but her own weight and felt guilty for it.

At the mouth of the cave, Bob paused to check the readings on his CO_2 monitor. "Oxygen's stable," he said. "Temperature's holding steady at fifty-two. Should be fine."

"Should be," Tanya muttered. "Famous last words."

Ellen clicked on her headlamp, the beam cutting a clean path into the darkness. "Let's get him out before something else goes wrong."

They entered single file, stooping through the serpentine tunnel, each echo bouncing ahead like ghosts of their footsteps. Ellen felt the air grow colder as they descended, and with it came that familiar charge—a tingling at the base of her neck, a knowing. Sawyer was awake.

The chamber opened around them like a cathedral carved by time. The new collapse lay still and pale under their lights, though altered from where Kirby had been extricated. New support beams, courtesy of Colton and Reese, secured the ceiling. Bob's team set to work with quiet efficiency, marking grids, unfurling tarps, and laying out brushes, trowels, and bone bags with the care of surgeons preparing an operating table.

Ellen kept her flashlight steady, watching the dust rise in ghostly spirals.

"Remember," Bob told his assistants, "we're focused on the human remains first. Then, we'll work on the artifacts."

"Looks like you've already exposed most of them," Mel put in.

"Yes," Bob acknowledged.

"But we have to be sure we get all of him out," Ellen warned, knowing the salting and burning wouldn't banish the vengeful spirit otherwise.

Aaron nodded, though he was ignorant of the reason, already brushing away loose sediment near the edge of the mound.

As she gingerly held the femur, Mel gasped softly, reverently. "He's young."

Bob leaned close. "Fifteen, maybe sixteen. This is our Sawyer."

A whisper brushed against Ellen's ear. *Leave me.*

She froze. The others hadn't heard it, but Sue's head jerked up anyway, as though she'd felt the same drop in temperature.

Tanya rubbed her arms. "It's colder all of a sudden."

Aaron frowned. "I thought it was just me."

Bob straightened, scanning the walls. "We're fine. Probably an airflow pocket."

Ellen knew better. She felt it pressing around her like fog, drawing closer with every scrape of a trowel. The cave itself seemed to shiver—the faint clink of rocks shifting in their sleep.

"Bob," she said, voice low but firm, "tell them to hurry."

He looked at her for half a beat, reading more than her words, then nodded. "Work fast, but careful."

Mel's brush danced faster over the soil. Aaron lifted another rock, revealing a cluster of small bones—a hand, fingers curled inward. "Almost got him," Aaron said softly. "Almost—"

The light above them flickered.

Ellen's breath caught. "Sawyer," she said, keeping her voice calm, motherly. "You don't need to stop us. We're helping you."

A metallic clang broke her sentence—the sound of a tool being flung across stone. Aaron jumped back as his trowel skittered past his boot and slammed into the wall behind him.

"I didn't drop that," he said.

Mel's flashlight flicked off. "I put new batteries in this thing."

"That's . . . odd." Sue met the concerned looks from her friends.

Then the smell hit—smoke and gunpowder and something older, like scorched iron. It filled Ellen's lungs, sharp and acrid, dragging her straight back to the moment Kirby's gun had fired.

She turned in a slow circle, scanning the shadows, no longer concerned about sparing the graduate students the truth. "Sawyer, listen to me. We are helping you to move on. You have no idea how much better you'll feel once you're at peace with Alf and Louisa."

"What's she talking about?" Aaron asked the professor.

"They're ghost hunters," Bob said flatly. "Just let them do their thing while we do ours."

The darkness thickened in one corner of the chamber, forming a silhouette—tall for a boy, shoulders narrow, features flickering between solid and not. His eyes burned like twin coals, rimmed with sorrow.

"Leave me," the voice rasped, shaking dust from the ceiling.

Mel backed toward the tunnel. "I—I think I'll wait outside."

Bob nodded. "Suit yourself. Aaron, why don't you follow her."

"No way," he said, eyes wide as quarters. "I find this fascinating, Professor."

"Suit yourself," he said again as Mel clambered from the cave.

The ghost boy's image wavered. The coins on the debris pile rattled. A gust of freezing air surged across the cavern, slamming into Ellen hard enough to make her stumble. Sue caught her elbow.

"Enough!" Sue shouted. "We're not thieves, Sawyer! We're trying to give you peace!"

The wind stopped. The lights flickered again, then steadied. The boy's form shrank slightly, wavering as if unsure.

Bob crouched by the remains. "I think he's testing us," he said softly. "Making sure we'll be respectful."

"Then let's prove him right," Ellen said through clenched teeth. "Hurry."

They worked faster. Piece by piece, they lifted what was left of Sawyer from the earth—skull, ribs, femur, fragments of vertebrae—all catalogued and photographed. As each piece was lifted, the pressure in the air seemed to build, as if the cave resented the theft of its ward.

Nearly an hour had passed when Bob finally straightened, holding the last small fragment—a phalange, twisted and blackened by time. "That's it," he said. "He's complete."

"Then let's move," Sue urged. "Now."

They gathered the evidence crates and began the slow retreat through the tunnel. Ellen went last, heart hammering. Behind her, the ghost's shape loomed again, larger now, angrier—or maybe just desperate.

"Please," she whispered. "We'll take care of you. I promise."

A rock hurled itself from the wall, exploding into dust at her feet. The tunnel filled with an echoing cry that wasn't rage so much as anguish, the sound of a life that had waited too long to be acknowledged.

"Go!" Bob shouted. "Everyone out!"

They stumbled into daylight, bursting from the cave like survivors from another century. Ellen turned just in time to see a swirl of shadow spill out behind them, dissolving in the sun's reach like smoke doused by rain.

"Accelerant," Tanya gasped, pulling a canister from her pack.

Sue tore open the bags containing the bones, setting them in the empty wheelbarrow. The remains gleamed pale and fragile in the light.

"Do it," Ellen said.

Tanya doused the bones with the accelerant while Sue lit a match.

Ellen sprinkled salt in a careful spiral while murmuring the words she'd learned through years of ghost crossings—an incantation as much prayer as command, "From earth you came, to light return. By flame and salt, by peace hard-earned. Rest, Sawyer, and be free."

"This is for Jason Albright." Sue dropped the match. Flames whooshed up from the wheelbarrow, startlingly bright against the gray afternoon. The wind carried the scent of salt and bone and release. The fire burned fast, consuming everything in less than five minutes, leaving only ash and heat and silence.

The air lightened.

For the first time in weeks, the forest felt alive again—the chirp of birds returning, the steady breath of the wind threading through cedar branches. The oppressive pressure that had haunted the area since their first arrival was gone.

Bob stood with his hat in hand, his eyes reflecting both awe and disbelief. "Well," he said softly. "That was something."

Ellen exhaled, her entire body trembling now that the danger had passed. "He's gone."

Sue squeezed her shoulder. "Not gone. Released."

Mel rubbed her arms, gooseflesh rising. "I don't know what that was, but I'm not sure they cover it in grad school."

Bob smiled faintly. "They should."

Ellen leaned against her cane. "We'll bury him properly," she said. "With a headstone. We'll pray for his redemption."

Bob looked down at her, respect softening his usual analytical gaze. "You think that matters?"

"It's all that matters," she said simply. "He was lost. Now he can find his way."

They waited for the ashes to cool.

Sue scooped them into a bag and sealed it. "Site's yours again, Professor. He won't be haunting it anymore."

Bob nodded, tucking his notebook into his vest. "Then we can finish what we started—quietly this time."

He and his team returned to the cave to excavate the artifacts.

As Ellen and her friends started up the trail toward their Chevy Onix, Sue carrying the sealed bag of a lost boy, the forest whispered around them—a rustle like a sigh, or maybe a thank you. Ellen glanced back once, toward the dark mouth of the cave. For a heartbeat, she saw him: a boy of fifteen, faint and luminous, standing in the shadow line between day and night. He raised his hand in farewell.

Ellen lifted hers in answer. Then he was gone, leaving only sunlight on stone.

CHAPTER TWENTY-THREE

The Crossing

Three days after Sawyer's cremation at Murder Rocks, Ellen parked beside Sue's Victorian and stared at the house's transformation: fresh paint gleamed along the gables, the porch railings were mended, and the house seemed to be smiling over the hillside. Inside, the sound of hammers and saws had given way to quieter rhythms—brushes sweeping dust, a vacuum's hum, the low murmur of men installing light fixtures and tile.

Down the hill, in the direction of the woods, a pair of survey flags still marked the spot where Bob Brooks and his graduate assistants had worked each day. Now the site stood empty. The excavation was complete, the report filed, and the cave system sealed for safety.

Bob was leaning against his pickup when Ellen arrived. He looked tired but satisfied, his khaki field clothes streaked with dust and coffee stains.

"Well, Professor?" Ellen asked. "Are we officially out of treasure?"

He smiled faintly. "As out as we can be. We finished the last sweep yesterday. Nothing left but limestone and time."

"Any doubt they were Sawyer's remains?" Tanya asked.

"I think the peace and quiet speaks volumes, don't you?" He lifted a folder from the passenger seat and tapped it. "Fifteen years old, give or take a few months. Growth plate evidence matches that age, and the dental work—or lack thereof—fits mid-nineteenth century. We also found fibers from a wool uniform coat and a bullet lodged near his ribs. My guess is he was hit by falling rock and debris when the ceiling came down."

Ellen's throat tightened. "Poor boy. He survived the war just to die in a hole."

Bob nodded. "But, if you're right, he carried the sense of purpose he had in life to his grave."

"Unfortunately, he carried it too far," Tanya put in. "Turning him vengeful."

Sue joined them on the porch, wiping her hands on her jeans. "Did you tell Ellen about the rest of it?"

"The rest?" Ellen asked.

Bob's eyes twinkled. "Gold bars, silver ingots, some minted coins dated 1858 to 1863. Alf Bolin wasn't just hiding pocket change. We're talking Confederate and Union payroll treasure, likely stolen from transports."

Tanya shifted her weight where they stood together near the pickup. "No wonder Sawyer guarded it like a dragon."

Sue folded her arms. "And since the cave is under my property line, it's legally ours."

Bob raised his brows. "I confirmed that with the county clerk this morning. Congratulations, ladies. You're officially land-rich, treasure-rich, and ghost-free—a rare combination."

Ellen laughed softly. "You make it sound so ordinary."

He smiled. "Ordinary's just history you haven't read yet."

As Bob and his team climbed into the cab of the pickup, he added, "After we're done cataloging them, I'll get these artifacts to a company I work with called Heritage Auctions and get back with you on the numbers. Thanks for sharing part of the bounty with me, Sue."

"No, thank *you*, Bob," Sue insisted. "We couldn't have done this without you."

"And Merry Christmas," Ellen added.

"Merry Christmas," Bob said with a wave.

The county cemetery sat on a low hill overlooking the White River, the late-autumn sky streaked with gold and lavender. Ellen stood between Sue and Tanya, the three of them bundled in coats, while the peaks of the Ozarks watched from the horizon.

They had prepared the ground themselves: a modest grave at the edge of the older section where Civil War markers dotted the grass. A small granite headstone waited at the foot of the open plot. The inscription read simply:

Sawyer

Friend to Alf Bolin

CA. 1849 – 1864

Ellen held a clay urn they'd purchased from an antique store on the Branson strip. It now contained Sawyer's ashes. Finally free of her cane, she set it gently in the grave and stepped back.

Tanya unfolded a small notecard. "I wrote something," she said, clearing her throat. "'For the boy who kept his promise: May the ground that hid you become the sky that frees you. May loyalty lead you home.'" Her voice quavered but did not break. She tucked the card into the soil.

Sue added a single silver coin from the trove—one of the cleaned pieces stamped 1861. "For luck in the next life."

Ellen stooped beside the grave, sprinkling a line of salt in a slow circle before covering the urn with the first handful of dirt. "Salt to purify," she murmured, "and earth to seal." She felt the faintest tremor in the air—not cold, not wind, but a presence.

They worked together until the grave was filled, smoothing the mound and setting the headstone in place. Then Ellen lit a small white candle and placed it before the stone.

"Sawyer," she said softly, "you've done enough guarding. It's time to rest."

The flame flickered, bent sideways, and steadied again. Ellen said a silent prayer for Jason Albright and the other victims of Sawyer and Alf Bolin's gang.

A shimmer passed through the air, faint but unmistakable, like heat rising from pavement or the shimmer of light on water. In that wavering brightness, Ellen glimpsed two figures: the boy in his threadbare coat and the young woman with red hair streaming behind her. They stood hand in hand, smiling. Then they turned and walked toward the sinking sun, fading as they went.

Tanya exhaled shakily. "You saw that too, right?"

Ellen nodded, unable to speak.

Sue dabbed at her eyes with the sleeve of her coat. "I suppose he suffered long enough in death to find his redemption, especially after such a hard life."

"I hope so," Tanya whispered.

When the last light left the sky, they blew out the candle and walked back to the Chevy Onix. The air felt lighter, the world quieter. No whisper followed them, no weight pressed against their shoulders.

As they drove away, Ellen looked back once more. The candle's wick still glowed faintly in the dusk, like a promise kept.

That night, Ellen found herself returning to the dark trail to Murder Rocks alone, surrounded by mist. It wasn't the dense, stifling kind she'd known in haunted places, but something weightless, luminous—moonlight turned to breath. The air smelled faintly of lilacs and river water. Somewhere unseen, a whippoorwill sang.

Ahead of her stretched a narrow dirt road lined with wildflowers—something she hadn't noticed before. Their colors glowed unnaturally bright, as if painted onto the fog. At the far end stood a small white farmhouse with smoke curling from its chimney. A lantern burned in the window—steady, golden, welcoming.

Was she still on Sue's land? Or had she somehow veered off too far?

Confused and lost, Ellen walked toward it, barefoot, the ground cool and soft beneath her feet. *Why am I barefoot?* she wondered. As she neared the farmhouse, she saw a young woman seated on the porch steps. Her hair was the color of corn silk, braided loosely over one shoulder, and her hands rested on her lap. Her eyes were pale—not blue, but a cloudy, silvery gray that seemed to look through rather than at. Yet when she turned her head toward Ellen, her smile was certain.

"You came," the woman said softly.

Ellen stopped at the foot of the steps. "You were expecting me? Who are you?"

"Annabel," the woman replied. "You've done what I could not. You freed him."

Ellen's throat tightened with understanding. She was talking to a ghost. "Sawyer?"

"Alf," Annabel said. "My brother has been restless all these long years. He blamed himself for leaving Sawyer in the dark. Now he can rest."

The words felt like a warm blanket, and yet Ellen's eyes stung. "He was just a boy," she whispered. "They both were."

Annabel rose. Though she moved carefully, as if still feeling her way through the world, there was grace in her motions, the surety of someone guided by more than sight. She reached out, and when her fingers brushed Ellen's hand, warmth bloomed there—not heat, but peace, radiating outward.

"You and your friends saw what others could not," Annabel said. "And you listened when the dead wept. Do you know how rare that is?"

Ellen shook her head, tears sliding down her cheeks. "We just wanted to help."

Annabel smiled again, tilting her face slightly toward the sound of Ellen's voice. "That's all Heaven ever asks."

The air shimmered, and for an instant Ellen thought she saw two figures in the distance—a boy and a red-haired girl, hand in hand, walking along the riverbank. Annabel turned toward them, her face glowing with serenity. "They're safe now," she said. "Home."

Ellen tried to ask if Annabel would go to them, but her voice caught. The mist began to dissolve, the edges of the dream brightening like sunrise peeking over the horizon.

Annabel's hand lingered in Ellen's a moment longer.

"Thank you," Annabel said. "May your heart always find the lost."

And then she was gone—the house, the mist, the song of the whippoorwill—all melting into the faint sound of morning wind against the windowpane.

Ellen woke in her Branson condo with tears on her face and moonlight pooling across the sheets. For a long time, she lay still, listening to Sue's rhythmic snores and the thrum of the noise machine. Gratitude overwhelmed her in that moment as more tears streamed from the corners of her eyes. She was grateful to have been given the privilege—and that's what it was, a privilege—to help the lost to find their way. Witnessing their peace ranked up there with seeing each of her babies for the first time. Joy and awe moved through her, and it was a long time before she found sleep again.

CHAPTER TWENTY-FOUR

Giants and Grace

As Ellen's flight touched down in San Antonio, the cold caves of Murder Rocks felt like they belonged to another lifetime. The December sun was warmer here, the light softer, and though she couldn't smell it now in the plane, she knew the air would carry the faint smell of mesquite.

Brian met her at the baggage claim, wrapping her in a hug that melted away weeks of tension. "You look like a woman who's wrestled the devil and won," he said.

"Close," she answered with a laugh.

Sue and Tanya followed them to Brian's SUV, and even though the three friends were tired, they seemed to get a second wind as they recounted parts of the trip to Brian as he drove them home.

After dropping off her friends, Ellen was delighted when she walked through the door of her own home to find the tree already up and twinkling beside the fireplace. Two days later, her kids and grand-kids arrived for Christmas Eve dinner, which Brian arranged to have catered this year. Nolan teased Ellen her for "ghost-hunting again" while she deflected with stories about geology and Civil-War research, something Lane was interested in. Alison, who'd recently come out to the family, brought her girlfriend to meet them for the first time, and Ellen was grateful that her daughter had someone special to celebrate the holidays with.

When Ellen placed the single silver coin from Sawyer's trove inside a glass ornament and hung it near the top of the tree, she caught Brian watching her.

"You're keeping that one?" he asked.

"I bought an ornament in Branson, but this will make a lovely memory."

Down the street, Sue hosted her family's traditional Christmas Eve surrounded by her children and grandchildren, while, on the other side of the neighborhood, Tanya spent the holiday with her husband and adult children, who insisted on hearing "the real ghost story of Branson." The three friends sent texts throughout the weekend—photos of family celebrations, recipes, and inside jokes about what they were going to do with their share of Alf Bolin's loot, though they were waiting to hear what the final numbers were.

For the first time in weeks, they slept soundly.

Two days after Christmas, Ellen stood at the window, coffee in hand, watching rain slide down the glass. She thought of the cave sealed beneath Missouri soil, of the boy at peace at last. The world felt balanced again.

When Sue called that evening, her voice was bright. "New Year's in Branson, as promised, for the final walkthrough with Caleb. The husbands are coming this time. I just purchased our tickets to *David* online."

Ellen smiled. "I can't wait, Sue. See you soon."

Branson glittered beneath frost and neon when they returned. The air smelled of cedar and wood smoke; downtown was strung with lights like a crown. Ellen and Brian, Sue and Tom, and Tanya and Dave took their seats inside the massive theater where *David* was about to begin.

From the moment the orchestra swelled and the first enormous figure stepped onto the stage—thirty feet tall, arms controlled by black-clad actors wielding long poles—the audience gasped. The giants moved with eerie grace, their shadows dwarfing the smaller players. Real sheep bleated at the edges of the stage while a harp's notes shimmered through the air.

Ellen felt the hairs rise on her arms. David's courage, the impossible odds, the single stone that toppled a monster—every beat mirrored the memory of Murder Rocks: the darkness, the danger, the moment when faith and friendship had stood against greed and violence.

She glanced at Sue and Tanya. Sue's hand found Tom's; Tanya wiped at her eyes. When the giants fell and the theater erupted in applause, Ellen leaned close to Brian and whispered, "That's how it felt below Murder Rocks, like we'd slayed a giant."

He kissed her temple. "You three have always had good aim."

Outside afterward, snow began to drift down, the flakes soft and slow as confetti.

"Who's up for Paula Deen's Gooey Butter Cake?" Sue asked as they walked toward their rental van in the parking lot.

"You had me at Paula Deen," Dave replied with a laugh.

Warm light spilled through the restored windows when they arrived at Sue's Victorian on Murder Ranch. Caleb opened the door with a flourish. "All yours, folks. She's ready for her close-up."

Inside, the house glowed—polished floors, fresh paint, the scent of lemon oil and cedar. The staircase gleamed, no longer creaking under invisible footsteps. The air felt still but alive, as if the walls themselves were exhaling relief.

Ellen ran her fingers along the banister. "Peaceful," she murmured.

Caleb nodded toward Brian. "Good to see you again, man. Your wife's got an eye for history."

Brian chuckled. "She's got a habit of bringing it home with her."

They laughed, wandering from room to room. Sue paused in the parlor, gazing at the mantle where a small, framed photograph of the headstone already stood.

"A tribute," Sue said. "To the boy who kept his promise."

They circled back to the entryway. The house felt complete—no whispers, no cold spots, only the steady hum of a new beginning. Outside, fireworks began to crackle across the hills.

Sue lifted her glass of sparkling cider. "To giants conquered," she said.

Ellen and Tanya clinked theirs to hers. "To giants conquered," they echoed.

Dave grinned. "And to whatever madness you three chase next."

"As long as it's not a casino," Tom said with a glance at Sue, a glance that might have been chastisement or playfulness. Ellen wondered if it was both in equal measure.

As if on cue, Sue's phone pinged with a new email. She glanced down, then looked up, eyes alight. "A query through the blog," she said. "A woman in Savannah, Georgia, needs our help."

Tanya groaned good-naturedly. "Couldn't even make it to midnight, could we?"

"What does she say?" Ellen looked over Sue's shoulder at the phone.

Sue scrolled through text and gave them the gist. "She's renovating a Victorian row house near Forsyth Park and claims that one of the walls in her parlor is weeping."

"Weeping?" Brain repeated.

"What does she mean?" Tom asked. "Does she describe it?"

Sue nodded. "She says that clear water seeps through the plaster, like tears, in the same place every night at midnight."

"Has she checked the plumbing?" Brian wanted to know.

"She says she's called three different plumbers, and they're all baffled," Sue replied.

Dave shook his head. "Probably a hoax. I would ignore it."

Tanya lightly punched Dave's shoulder. "After all I've witnessed, I think it's worth looking into."

Sue lifted her brow and her glass. "To Savannah next. Am I right?"

Ellen laughed, heart swelling with that familiar thrill—the promise of another mystery, another haunting, another chance to heal the past. "To Savannah next," she said.

The three glasses met in a bright chime as fireworks bloomed beyond the window, scattering color across the Victorian's polished walls. The light danced over their faces—three women who had faced darkness and had carried each other through it, ready once more to step into the unknown.

E P I L O G U E

Riches and Rest

Ellen was sorting through laundry in early February when her phone chimed with Sue's ringtone—a snippet of *Sweet Caroline* that reminded her of Sue's most spectacular karaoke performance. Ellen smiled, set the basket on the bed, and answered. "Hey, Sue. What's up?

"Check your email," Sue said, breathless. "Bob just sent the final figures."

"I'll bite," Ellen said, sitting on the edge of the bed. "How'd we do?"

A pause—then a laugh that sounded too big for one person. "You might want to sit down for this. Are you ready?"

"I'm ready."

"One million, sixty-eight thousand, two hundred and forty dollars."

Ellen blinked. "Say that again?"

"You heard me. Heritage Auctions just wired the funds to the escrow account. After Bob's cut and taxes, we each clear about two hundred fifty grand. Tanya's threatening to buy an RV for a national parks tour and is trying to get Dave on board."

Ellen chuckled. "That sounds like Tanya."

"Bob says the Springfield Museum exhibit's already underway," Sue went on. "They're calling it *Guardians of the Gold.* They've got our photo with him and the excavation team, and a whole section dedicated to Sawyer and Louisa. They've even partnered with Oakdale School for the Blind to display some of Alf's letters to Annabel. Visitors will be able to scan a QR code that links to the historical report."

Ellen's throat tightened. "That's wonderful news. I'm so glad that Sawyer and Louisa won't be forgotten."

"They won't," Sue said softly. "I'm glad we did it this way—clean, transparent, and legal. I didn't want a ghost of conscience haunting us next."

"No, I agree. Everything above board."

There was a short silence—comfortable, familiar.

"You know what's funny?" Sue said after a beat. "Even though I was desperate to find the treasure to make things up to Tom—you know, for losing forty-five grand at the casino—deep down, I was scared that I'd turn around and do the same thing—lose all my share of the loot."

"And you're not afraid of that anymore?"

"Last night, Tom suggested that we put it all in trust funds for the kids and grandkids, and I agreed." Sue sighed. "I really want to go back to the casino, don't get me wrong, but . . ." Sue's voice trailed off.

"But?" Ellen echoed.

"The longer I stay away, the more in control I feel."

"Oh, Sue! I'm so happy to hear you say that. Tanya and I have been so worried."

"I'm not saying I won't go back."

"Just not anytime soon, right?"

Sue paused for a long moment, and Ellen held her breath.

"Right, of course," Sue finally said.

Ellen smiled. "Besides, we've got another trip to plan."

"Indeed, we do. March in Savannah should be stunning," Sue pointed out. "Do you think we can be ready in a few weeks?"

"A few weeks? I think we can manage that," Ellen said as Moseby jumped beside her on the bed. "I might need to take Moseby along, though. He can sense that I'm planning something."

"Bring him. It'll be nice and warm, and he's a good little investigator."

"You hear that, Moseby?" Ellen said to her little, black dog. "Sue says you're a good little investigator!"

They ended the call. The room fell quiet again, save for the hum of the heater and Moseby licking the bedspread. Ellen looked at her phone, still glowing with the open email: *Heritage Auctions Final Statement.* Below the balance sheet was a note from Bob:

*For the record: Peace is worth more than gold. But this isn't bad, either. —
Bob B.*

Ellen smiled, closing the message. She kissed Moseby just as Brian came in with a grin.

"Are you really leaving again in three weeks?" he asked.

"Is that okay?" she asked with a frown.

He took her hands and pulled her to her feet before taking her into his arms. "Only if you promise to make up for lost time before you go."

Ellen leaned into him with a soft giggle. "That would be my pleasure."

Moseby chirped with a soft bark of jealousy, reminding them that he was in the room, too.

"Don't worry, Moseby," Brian said in a voice that was low and husky. "You'll get time with her, too, I'm sure."

Ellen met Brian's warm lips with hers and closed her eyes as joy and peace washed over her.

Tomorrow would bring new stories, new mysteries, maybe even a weeping wall—but today belonged to peace and to the living who had earned it.

***

THE END

Thank you for reading my story. I hope you enjoyed it! If you did, please consider leaving a review. Reviews help other readers to discover my books, which helps me.

Please visit my website at evapohler.com to get the next book, *The Weeping Wall.*

Here's the blurb:

A wall that weeps. A secret that kills.

When a new homeowner in Savannah, Georgia, writes to *Ghost Healers, Inc.* about a wall in her Victorian row house that "weeps" every night, Sue can't resist the call. Beneath the city's beauty—where moss drapes like mourning veils and whispers cling to every corner—Ellen, Sue, and Tanya uncover a haunting unlike any they've faced before.

What begins as a curious anomaly soon turns sinister as ghostly voices echo through the house and saltwater tears stain the plaster. The deeper the team digs, the more Savannah itself seems to resist them—its genteel charm hiding something rotten just below the surface.

In a city built on secrets, the line between the living and the dead blurs. Someone—or something—doesn't want the truth revealed. And as the haunting intensifies, Ellen, Sue, and Tanya realize that not all ghosts are trapped in the past.

Some still walk among them.

EVA POHLER

Eva Pohler is a *USA Today* bestselling author of over thirty novels in multiple genres, including mysteries, thrillers, and young adult paranormal romance based on Greek mythology. Her books have been described as "addictive" and "sure to thrill"—*Kirkus Reviews*.

To learn more about Eva and her books, and to sign up to hear about new releases, and sales, please visit her website at https://www.evapohler.com.

Acknowledgments

Many thanks to Woody P. Snow for his book *Murder Rocks: Alf Bolin and the Civil War,* on which much of the historical details in this novel about Alf Bolin and his gang are based.

I would like to thank the following premium members for their continued support:

Susan Albright

Amie Boutte

Lori Brooks

Kathy Cannarozzi

Debi Canon

Theresa Christ

Rebekka and Sherry Colegrove

Betty Downs

Amanda Ecker

Kerry Erickson

Venette Grisham

Samie Hall-Rood

Shellie Hedge

Michelle Holloway

Anita Klaboe

Leslie Lawrence

Carrie McCauley

Melissa Millar

Patrick Mitchell

Glorianna Murry

Diane Ortiz-Davis

Rachel Schmidt
Patricia Hand Salinas
Candy Smith
Debi Vap
Tammy Wojcik